BOOK ONE

CREATED
THE DEVIL'S APPRENTICE

GREGORY A. ROGERS

BOOK ONE

CREATED
THE DEVIL'S APPRENTICE

GREGORY A. ROGERS

Build. Buzz. Launch.
Media & Publishing
Dallas, TX

The Created Series:
CREATED: The Devil's Apprentice - Book One
Copyright © 2021 Gregory A. Rogers.

Published by BBL Publishing, an imprint of
Build.Buzz.Launch. Media & Publishing, Dallas TX, 75218
www.buildbuzzlaunch.com

First Edition
ISBN 978-0-9909725-8-7 Paperback
ISBN 978-1-7352966-4-7 ebook

Graphic Design: deLine and Co.
Cover illustrations: iStock Photo
Interior Cross illustrations after page 37 Courtesy: Freepix.com

Manufactured in the United States of America

For print copies, author interviews contact:
info@buildbuzzlaunch.com.

Dedicated To:
The God who created me, who saved me,
who sustains me and who one day will welcome
me back into His loving embrace.

To my wife, Amanda, and our sons, Ryan and Jackson,
who encouraged me to pursue this dream,
even when it seemed it would always be just beyond
my reach. Thanks for always believing in me.

Contents

Contents

INTRODUCTION

"In the beginning was the Word, and the Word was with God,
and the Word was God. He was in the beginning with God. All things
came into being through Him, and apart from Him, nothing
came into being that has come into being."

John 1:1–3

Before the beginning, there was only Him...Elohim. Besides Him, nothing else existed. No matter...no space...no semblance of time. He simply existed, having never experienced a beginning of His own nor known the limitations of time. From eternity past into eternity future, Elohim was, is, and always will be All-knowing, All-powerful, Perfect and Eternal...the One True God.

Yet, nothing with God is as simple as it seems. Though One in Essence, Elohim existed in the triune Personages of Yahweh, Yeshua, and Ruach Elohim, or as some call Them, God the Father, God the Son, and God the Holy Spirit—the Trinity. While He possessed no kingdom of any kind before His creation of heaven, the angels, and mankind, Elohim was, without question, Sovereign. With this simple existence, He was perfectly content. Perfect in every way.

So, why does a perfect God who knows all things create anything that has free will, and with it, the capacity to destroy His perfection? The answer to this question both shook and established the pillars of heaven and earth, forever shaping the course of all future events.

PROLOGUE

The Spiritual Realm of the Physical Earth: Present Day

Over the pine woods of Montana, the gray sky erupted in glowing streaks of fire. Beneath the display, flames torched the treetops which lined the banks of a small river as it snaked its way through the normally tranquil valley. On either side, steep cliffs rose into the sky, their rocky walls a blend of jagged crags and smooth boulders. Both were the product of the river's rushing waters. In the glow of the surrounding flames, the winged-silhouettes of angels and demons darted across what had become the newest battlefield in an ancient celestial war.

A glowing cinder floated on the breeze, dancing perilously close to the shallow pool in the riverbed where Corporal Gideon, a winged soldier, took refuge. The cinder was all that remained of Private Mordecai after he was struck by several flaming arrows. Above Gideon stretched the steep, tree-lined embankment over which the rest of his cohort took flight in a desperate attempt to escape the onslaught below. Screams from its lofty height were followed by a shower of cinders.

"Trapped," whispered Gideon as he hunkered down in an eddy behind a large boulder. Despite the arrows that landed all around him, his attention was momentarily drawn away from the spiritual realm in which he fought to the parallel physical realm of man. Gideon couldn't take his eyes off the peaceful scene which transpired just upstream…two fly fishermen were tossing their lines over the water, working to catch trout. The humans carried on, unaware that they stood in the middle of a celestial battlefield on which a cohort of God's army was being defeated by Satan's warriors.

A bright explosion brought Corporal Gideon's attention back to the spiritual realm and his need to focus on his own survival. Throughout the day's battle, he and his comrades had been driven up the riverbed. Now pressed against the embankment, large groups of angels fell prey to each fiery volley from the bows of the Fallen. It seemed only a matter of time before they would all feel the searing heat of a flaming arrow.

Downstream, amid the chaos of fire and smoke, Gideon spotted a group of young angel warriors, clearly lost and depleted from fighting.

Sergeant Josiah stood and spread his silver wings. "We have to get out of here. Follow me!" The commanding angel disappeared for a moment, then reappeared atop the steep embankment. He yelled down, "All clear. Hurry, move now!"

Weary warriors spirit-leaped to join their sergeant atop the embankment. The weaker angels reappeared in mid-air, desperately flapping their damaged wings to reach higher ground. Fire arrows whizzed through the air, most finding their targets. Those angels who were struck barely had time to express the agony of the moment before being obliterated. Those fortunate enough to make it to the top of the embankment spirit-leaped again, under orders to save themselves for a future fight.

Corporal Gideon tried to do the same, using all that remained of his energy. He vanished for only a moment before reappearing well short of the high embankment. Several fiery arrows grazed his side and wings, sending the young angel flipping upwards and downwards in a confusion of spinning river and trees. His flight ended when he crashed, face down in the waters he'd left only moments before. Looking up at the steep embankment, Corporal Gideon was overcome by the shrill screams and the shower of glowing cinders. He stammered, "They're all gone."

He whispered, "It's all been a trap. Satan's army must have driven us to this location, knowing eventually we would spirit-leap to the top. With little-to-no energy left, we'd be easy targets for their rested warriors."

Gideon wondered how any contingent could survive such an ambush, especially a new cohort just one day removed from basic training?

Alone in the darkness of enemy occupied space, Gideon remembered what his instructors at Camp Wisdom had taught him: *Life outside the light of Elohim was nothing but …*

He whispered to himself, "Weeping and gnashing of teeth."

Utter darkness descended around him. The luminescent blues and greens of plant life in the spiritual realm of the first heaven turned into lifeless husks devoid of color. Scorching heat bombarded his body from all sides, yet it didn't seem to come from the blazing fires set off by the enemy's weaponry. This was something different. Something driven by the evil which surrounded him.

Gideon grabbed his arm and side where flaming arrows had grazed him. His energy drained, he knew a spirit-leap back to base camp was impossible. Given what had just happened to his comrades who tried a shorter leap off the battlefield, perhaps his fatigue was a blessing.

A flaming arrow whizzed through the air inches from his head, then splashed in the water and smoldered.

Gideon heard voices coming from the woods above. Five angel warriors flew out of the smoke above the riverbed and landed in the shin-deep water beside the corporal.

Fear gave way to relief as Gideon recognized his tentmates. He whispered, "I thought you all were finished up there."

Private Luke said, "We almost were. Sergeant Josiah guided us all the way back to the edge.

Too bad he...Sarge didn't make it. He tried to go back for Nahum and Jezreel, but there were just too many demons. We're lucky the six of us are still in one piece."

"Any sign of Lieutenant Malachi?" Gideon asked.

The young warriors shook their heads, fear welling up in their eyes. All seemed lost.

* * * * * *

Lieutenant Malachi took a position high above the disputed space occupied by what remained of the lost unit of soldiers. All was ablaze except for down in the riverbed, where a few shallow pools of water offered refuge beneath the smoke. Using their swords and shields, the team of warriors had managed to expand their small pool into a makeshift trench system.

Still, if the enemy attacked from his vantage point, those angels would be easy targets.

Lieutenant Malachi scanned each tree above Gideon's position for any signs of the enemy. As suspected, three of Satan's dark-winged Fallen warriors moved deftly among the branches, maneuvering into position to finish the job on the six remaining warriors from Malachi's latest boot-camp class. The demons each raised a bow and nocked an arrow.

Instinctively, Malachi raised his own bow, nocking two arrows split between his fingers with a third clutched between his teeth. Without hesitation, he fired his first shot. Two arrows whistled through the air, each taking a separate path to its target. Two of the Fallen warriors burst into embers.

The third demon panicked. He spun, sighted Malachi, and raised his bow.

In one lightning-fast motion, Malachi's firing hand moved from the bowstring, nocked a third arrow, then fired. The arrow pierced the dark chest armor of the third Fallen warrior. There was a flash of fireworks, then nothing left of the demon but a shower of falling sparks.

Malachi spirit-leaped to the ravine below.

Corporal Gideon and the others, terrified and battle-shocked, looked to their lieutenant as their savior.

Malachi whispered, "It's time to fall back, warriors."

"But how?" asked Gideon. "The Fallen control the skies and the high ground at the top of that embankment. So, flying out of here seems impossible, and we don't have enough energy for a substantial spirit-leap."

Malachi thought for a moment, examining their position, looking for some means of escape. Finally, he whispered, "You're right, Corporal. Flying out of here is not an option. So, spirit leaping is our only viable choice. But, with no energy for large jumps, we must be strategic in the small leaps we are able to make."

Malachi reassuringly placed a hand on Gideon's shoulder and asked, "What do you see going back this way?" He pointed back up the riverbed in the direction from which they'd previously come.

One of the privates said, "Sir, that's the direction back into enemy occupied space. Shouldn't we be looking the opposite direction?"

Malachi answered, "Only if you don't want to make it back to camp tonight. Gideon, what do you see?"

Corporal Gideon squinted as he looked up the riverbed. All he could make out were flames dancing across the waters of the river, but there seemed no way to head in that direction without easily being detected by the enemy. He shook his head in frustration.

"All I can see is water, fire, and an enormous number of the enemy."

Malachi added, "Yes, but do you see those large mounds of branches on the edge of the river on the left shore? There. And, on the right shore over there?"

"Sure. They look like beaver lodges. I don't see how beavers can help us out of here."

Malachi responded, "They already have."

The six warriors stared up at their training officer, perplexed at what he could possibly mean by his comment. Finally, the lieutenant explained.

"Inside each of those beaver lodges is a sizable empty space, the beaver's den. With the outside of the lodges on fire, the heat of the blaze may conceal us if we were to spirit leap into each beaver den. Perhaps we could rest long enough to make several leaps in succession, using each beaver lodge as a sort of stepping stone through the enemy lines. Get far enough past their warriors, and we could likely wait long enough to restore our energy. We'd then be able to spirit leap to safety."

Dejected looks gave way to hope. Moments later, Malachi ordered the small group to make the spirit leap within the closest beaver lodge. Once inside, Malachi's suspicions proved correct. Though enemy warriors could be heard just feet away outside the beaver lodge, the heat of the fire burning the roof of the structure concealed the presence of angelic host hiding within. Four similar leaps later, the small band of angels was able to rest. Once recovered, they made a final spirit leap back to base camp. Though they'd always listened to Malachi as their boot camp trainer, they now had an entirely new level of respect for his wisdom and abilities.

* * * * * *

Upon arrival at base camp, Corporal Gideon and his tentmates were surprised to find the rest of the cohort there, battered but intact. Even Sergeant Josiah rested among the warriors, having clearly received medical attention.

Gideon asked Sergeant Josiah, "How is it possible you survived? After everyone spirit-leaped up the embankment, there were nothing but screams and a shower of ash. I was certain the Fallen had destroyed you."

Sergeant Josiah, still wearing his damaged breastplate, shook his head. "Well, we got ambushed, and Satan's warriors took out many of our number, but what the Fallen—and we—didn't know was that Lieutenant Malachi was setting his own trap. As soon as they moved to finish us, the lieutenant was on them."

One after the other, members of the cohort shared their own personal experience of how Lieutenant Malachi had intervened to snatch them from certain defeat. Though there were reasons to celebrate their escape, many of the young warriors were despondent, questioning their preparedness for combat. Beginning as a low murmur, their contagious fear spread like fire through the cohort.

Corporal Gideon turned to his left, expecting to continue his conversation with a tentmate.

Instead, he came face-to-face with Lieutenant Malachi. The dark-skinned angel, wearing the golden armor of an officer in the Army of the Host, looked unshaken compared to the rest of the warriors.

Lieutenant Malachi eyed each of the scared young soldiers. "So, you doubt yourselves now that you've tasted combat for the first time?"

"Sir, we aren't like you," Gideon said. "God made you for this. We were made for service and peaceful worship. There is no chance any of us will get through this war without suffering unimaginable pain."

"Do you really believe I am so different from each of you?" Lieutenant Malachi asked. "True, I have experienced more combat, and that gives me an advantage. But I started much further behind than many of you. Before Satan's dark angels fell, before all this chaos in the lower heavens, I was not a warrior. I was naïve and uncertain in my choices. I was torn between loyal service to our King and serving my own self-interests. In fact, I sometimes still wonder if I am worthy of being in the King's service. Perhaps I deserve to be listed among the ranks of the Fallen. Since I remain in His service, I will protect Elohim's servants from Satan's wrath. I will do it no matter what it may cost me."

Private Jonah burst into the conversation. "Why is it that any of us must fight? Satan and mankind brought on this war. Not us. If God had only refrained from creating mankind, Satan and the Fallen may have never rebelled. Without mankind, there would be no reason to wage war with the Fallen angels. Let them have this lower heaven. We could just remain in the higher heavens. But because Elohim created mankind and now wants to save them, we get to suffer."

Malachi removed his sword and sheath from around his waist and placed it on his satchel.

He paced back and forth in front of the warriors, scratching his chin. Then he said, "So, I guess you wonder why God created man. Right?"

"Yes," answered Gideon, "having done so has created many problems for the King, as well as us who have devoutly followed Him."

"Well, yes and no," said Malachi. "Certainly, mankind fell and Elohim knew in advance they would. So, I understand why one might question the wisdom in such a move. I once did. To properly understand why we fight as we do, you must first understand what really happened before *in the beginning*. When you do, you will see the source of our eternal conflict is not found in the King's creation of man, but in His creation of all of us. The fall of heaven's celestial beings started billions of years ago, when I was a young angel ..."

CHAPTER ONE

THE MENTOR

*"You had the seal of perfection, full of wisdom and perfect in beauty.
You were in Eden, the garden of God; every precious stone
was your covering: the ruby, the topaz and the diamond, the beryl,
the onyx and the jasper; the lapis lazuli, the turquoise and
the emerald; and the gold, the workmanship of your settings and sockets,
was in you. On the day that you were created. They were perfect."*

Ezekiel 28:12b-13

Eternity Past in the Heavenly Realm...
Before *In the Beginning*

The gate creaked as it swung on its hinges, an irritating noise penetrating the serenity of Eden. Malachi cringed and then knelt to examine the source of the offense. His knee pressed deeply into the feathery grass which surrounded the entryway into this greatest garden of God.

Never had Malachi known anything in Elohim's heavenly kingdom to emit such an unholy sound.

Perplexed, the young angel closed and then slowly reopened the gate. It creaked again. He whispered, "I don't understand."

"Haven't you seen a gate before?" asked a voice.

Malachi spun on his knee to face two approaching angels. He shrugged and answered, "Of course I've seen a gate, but did you hear that sound?"

"What sound?" asked the other angel.

Malachi gave the gate another gentle push. It emitted the same drawn-out creak.

The two angels covered their ears just as Malachi had done when he first opened the gate. The trio began to scour the entrance, searching for the cause of the grating sound. All that stood out was the beauty and artistry captured in the gate's form; a golden frame laced with diamond flakes glistening amid the ever-present glory of the King. As for the creaking sound—that would remain a mystery as the three angels gave up their search and returned to their reason for coming to the garden in the first place.

They introduced themselves to one another. Bartholomew, a short angel with stubby gray wings, was just as wide as he was tall. His curly beard only enhanced his square shape, hiding what little neck he did have and making his head seem to protrude only slightly above his shoulders.

Alexander, a giant of an angel, completely dwarfed Bartholomew and even stood nearly a head above the six-foot-four-inch Malachi. Alexander's chiseled face, broad shoulders and magnificent silver wings made him look more like one of the garden's numerous statues than one of its guests. Malachi, the youngest of the three angels, possessed a muscular build and broad wings with shimmering white feathers. While the other two angels had fair skin, Malachi was dark-complected. His most prominent feature, his bald head, was the perfect canvas on which to show off his ebony skin.

Alexander eyed Malachi suspiciously. "So, besides being the cause of the first imperfect thing in heaven, what brings you to the back part of Eden?"

The two angels laughed.

Malachi ignored the joke at his expense. "Actually, I'm supposed to be assigned my mentor today."

"Us too," said Bartholomew.

He and Alexander reached into the satchels which hung around their waists, producing the same invitation as Malachi's. Each invitation was a work of art. Made of the finest papyrus, hand-scribed by an elder angel's hand, the scrolls shimmered with gold and pearl. Malachi unraveled his own scroll. An invitation of this type had to be from an angel in the first sphere.

"Do you know who sent it?" asked Malachi.

Bartholomew shook his head. "No, it's anonymous. Just says it's from 'Your Potential Mentor.' I'm beginning to wonder if it was such a good idea to come chasing this thing down. After all, it does say another mentor awaits us at the Quad, should we decide to forgo this option."

"And just think of what we're missing," Alexander said. "All of the festivities associated with this ritual are happening right now back at the Quad. If we're going to do this, let's get going. Maybe we can make it back before the ceremony is over." He pushed the creaking gate aside and rushed on, unperturbed by its intrusion into paradise.

The noise sent a startled flock of ruby-breasted tsee-Pohr into flight and launched Bartholomew off like a flaming arrow from a bow. As the stout angel began his pursuit of Alexander, he looked back at Malachi, who remained at the gate.

"Come on. What are you waiting for?"

Malachi gave the gate one more curious shove.

The grating sound vibrated down his back and ruffled his wing feathers. Shaking his head, he took off after the other two. The strange creaking carried on the wind. He dared look over his shoulder. Behind him, the swinging gate squeaked a few more times, then slammed shut.

******

To Malachi's surprise, the trail they took lacked the normal grooming he was accustomed to seeing throughout the kingdom. In fact, the farther he followed it, the more overgrown with vegetation the trail became. Before long, he could hardly make out the path at all, and every step became a hurdle in a celestial obstacle course.

More than once, Malachi peered over his shoulder and considered turning back. Each time, though, he weighed the consequences of giving up too soon. *What will I say to my superiors if they ask how things went with my new mentor? That I quit searching because I couldn't find my way through a few shrubs? That might blemish my record and set me back on future advancements. No, this has to be a test of some sort.*

Malachi pressed forward. Still, every step through the tangled mesh of undergrowth challenged his will.

"This is as far as I go," panted Bartholomew as he retraced his steps. "I can't see how this can be worth it. I'm sure another mentor will be just as capable of helping me reach my next rank."

"Where's Alexander?" asked Malachi.

"He kept running...even when I told him to slow down and wait for us."

Malachi ran his hands over some vines that blocked the path. "Doesn't this all seem strange to you?"

"I don't know if 'strange' is the right word for it. I was thinking, 'unnecessary.'"

Malachi pulled out his invitation again. "Why would anyone choose to send us through this tangled thicket to get to our meeting site? After all, the Department of Angelic Advancement's instructions to all other apprentice angels were so straightforward and sensible."

Malachi read from the standard invitation, "'Meet your mentor at the Quad in front of the DoAA building with everyone else and their new mentors. Join the group as we celebrate experienced angels helping younger ones grow in faithful service to our King.'"

Bartholomew could manage only an exasperated sigh in response as he continued to trudge back to the exit.

Malachi looked again at the alternative invitation the three of them had chosen to pursue. It stated:

Meet your special mentor by way of entrance through the east side of Eden. There, you will find a gate and a path. Continue on the path regardless of the challenges, and at the end, it will be clear to my true protégé where I will be. If you find you are not up to the task, then meet your original mentor with the rest of the eligible candidates back at the Quad in front of the DoAA.

The more Malachi thought about the instructions, the more insensible they seemed. Why would this potential mentor keep his identity a secret? None of it made any sense. Yet, a voice from within urged him on.

Finally, the young angel broke free from the jungle. Through the surrounding canopy, a radiant light appeared focused with unusual intensity on one spot in particular—a small, rundown cabin in the middle of the clearing. As he neared the structure, he noticed Alexander standing to his left, apparently assessing the situation.

Compared to the thick vegetation surrounding the cabin, the grounds in the clearing were almost barren. Rust-colored dirt extended away from the run-down building, without even the simplest of paths beckoning guests to its small front porch.

"Have you checked to see if anyone is there?" Malachi asked Alexander.

"Why should we? No one associated with the mentorship program would ever choose a place like that as the site of our first meeting. I say we keep going."

"To where?" asked Malachi. "The instructions say to follow the path to the rendezvous point. There is nothing after that. Let's see if this is the right place."

"You can waste your time if you want, but I'm moving on." Alexander raced off past the cabin, diving again into the formidable jungle on the opposite side of the clearing.

Malachi studied the weathered cabin and the unusual nature of the grounds where it was located. The closer he looked, the more Malachi could see that the red dirt surrounding the structure was the least disturbing feature. Trees at the edges of the clearing were twisted and gnarled. Some had branches which grasped around the trunks of neighboring trees; others had roots thrusting out of the ground and then clawing at the soil deeper in the jungle. It was as if the trees were trying to pull themselves away from the run-down structure at the center of the clearing. It was hard to believe that a part of Eden could be so devoid of God's perfection. Yet again, a voice from within compelled Malachi to explore this place.

He stepped onto the front porch; his eyes were drawn to the ground where a brilliant light creeped beneath the doorway. Normally, he felt at peace moving anywhere in Elohim's Kingdom.

Yet, something about this small cabin produced a strange sensation that rippled down his back and caused his wings to flap nervously.

Malachi knocked, uncertain of who or what awaited him on the other side.

As he waited for a response, his attention was captured by even more unsettling sights and sounds. Several *shoo-AHLs* scurried along the ground near Malachi's feet, their soft red fur matted and disheveled. These small rodent-like creatures normally produced a melodious sound as communication took place between members of the herd. For some reason, this group seemed strangely out of tune, and the synchronization of their movements was off. As Malachi watched the herd chaotically stumble over one another, moving past him in rolling waves of fur, he was startled by a deep voice calling out to him from within the cabin. "Enter, Malachi. I've been waiting for you."

Slowly, Malachi turned the doorknob and pushed open the door. It too creaked, just like the gate. Before he had a chance to contemplate it further, his eyes were drawn to the unmistakable glow of resplendent glory dancing across the floor, its source emanating from a back room.

Confusion gave way to astonishment as his host and potential mentor stepped into view.

Malachi didn't know how to react. What should one do when meeting the *Angel of Light* for the first time?

Malachi kneeled. "Blessed beyond measure."

Lucifer responded, "Oh yes, blessed beyond ..." then stopped and cleared his throat. He continued, "Hello, Malachi. I'm glad you saw fit to persevere through the rigors and uncertainty of this trek. Few angels have been given this opportunity, and you are the first to make it to this rendezvous point."

Malachi said, "I had no idea. The associate at the Department of Angelic Advancement wouldn't tell me who I would be meeting. Your identity, I mean. They said they couldn't share that with me in advance...based on your orders."

"Ever since I was made this garden's Overseer, my schedule has become packed. In order to participate in the mentorship program, I have to be sure the angel I select as my charge is just as committed to the process as I am. To test the resolve of each potential protégé, I set up challenges such as finding this cabin. Unfortunately, it has been a long time since an angel continued all the way through to completion."

Malachi felt privileged, but also wondered why the most prominent angel in all of heaven would choose him as an apprentice.

******

Lucifer was different from the other angels, having been fashioned by Elohim with special care. He was beyond flawless. He was sealed with perfection.

Though slight in frame compared to other high-ranking angels, Lucifer still possessed a muscular form, his white wings serving as the perfect backdrop for the artistry of all that he was. His radiance and beauty exceeded even the Seraphim, the angelic class who directly served Elohim on the Holy Mount. All paled in comparison.

While Lucifer's beauty was unmatched by any angel, this fact wasn't the only reason the King bestowed upon him the title of "Angel of Light." For billions of years, Lucifer served Elohim with distinction, honoring the King in every conceivable manner. Eventually, it was this outstanding performance which earned him a promotion to the premier assignment in all the heavens, short of placement on the Holy Mount. Lucifer was made Overseer of the Garden of Eden.

During his time in the position, Lucifer worked diligently to enhance the beauty of Elohim's original creation, with its lush vegetation, four flowing rivers, and at its center, the Tree of Life.

Lucifer's role involved cultivating the many kinds of vegetation and caring for the numerous statues found across its sizeable landscape. New hybrid plants were introduced and presented in elaborate beds. Water features were added, as well as ornamental displays emphasizing different aspects of the King's character.

With each new arrangement, statue, and display, the King received even greater glory and praise. This was enhanced by the many extraordinary songs of worship Lucifer composed and performed for all who came to honor their King. It was a position that gave Elohim's greatest created being even more opportunities to bring glory to his Creator. The Angel of Light made the most of each opportunity, worshipping and serving the King with great fervor whenever possible.

******

Malachi, still recovering from the shock of learning Lucifer had requested him as his charge, said, "I can't believe you would even participate in the mentorship program."

Lucifer grinned. "I find it to be an important step for angels who have a lot of potential, angels such as yourself. I had no doubt it would be you who would make it all the way here; you who would become my latest protégé."

Malachi couldn't believe his ears. The Angel of Light thought he had a lot of potential. Curiosity overcame him. "May I ask, Sir, why you invited me?"

"I've had my eyes on you for quite some time, Malachi, ever since the King said what He did about you on your creation day."

"Sir, what do you mean?"

"No one has ever told you? On the day Elohim created you, He said you would be 'the One.'"

Malachi was more confused than ever. "What did the King mean by that?"

"No one knows, but I intend to find out. How would you feel about me helping you unravel this mystery?"

"I would be honored, Sir."

"My last charge started off calling me *Sir*. Though I don't want us to dispense with all formalities, do call me Lucifer."

"Of course, S . . . I mean Lucifer. You've mentioned your last charge a couple of times now.

Do you mind me asking you who that was?"

"I'm sure you're familiar with the Archangel Michael."

Malachi was speechless. To be considered to follow in the footsteps of one of the greatest archangels was more than humbling. Still, if this was the King's will, there was only one answer to give.

Malachi said, "Anything I can do to faithfully serve the King, I will do with all that is in me. Yes, I accept your mentorship."

"Good. Then my plans begin today." Looking past Malachi, Lucifer's attention drifted somewhere else as he grinned. Then, as if shaken back to reality from a dream, he said, "Certainly, I will show you how to faithfully serve the King, but I will also show you how to fulfill your own potential. Trust me when I say, 'You owe that much to yourself.'"

"Of course, I trust you to lead me. Thank you for the opportunity. Blessed beyond measure."

Lucifer stepped forward and placed his hand on Malachi's shoulder. As he did, the floorboards beneath their feet creaked as if the planks were about to break.

Lucifer shrugged and said, "Hmm . . . Blessed beyond measure. Let us begin."

CHAPTER TWO

BLESSED BEYOND MEASURE

"And God is able to bless you abundantly, so that in all things at all times,
having all that you need, you will abound in every good work."

2 Corinthians 9:8

Blessed *beyond measure. Blessed beyond measure.* These words, repeated by the angels in all six levels of heaven, served as more than just a greeting among the heavenly host. The words were a praise offering to their King, filling the air with a musical tone and a pleasing aroma.

Every thought. Every word. Every act of worship in the heavens focused on one point . . . the temple at the apex of everything Elohim created.

Radiant light draped the Holy Mount in unimaginable brilliance. It was here that Yahweh, the first Personage of the Trinity, received worship from those created specifically for that purpose. In a temple that was more light and energy than anything of substance, Yahweh made Himself present in the innermost chamber known as the Holy of Holies. Every angel was filled with awe and wonder as they contemplated the breadth and depth of their great God. In many ways, Elohim remained a mystery to them all, even to the Seraphim who served Him directly on the Holy Mount. After all, who can fully comprehend what it means to be perfect and eternal?

And who can truly fathom One Essence existing as Three Personages? Yet, such are innate characteristics of Elohim.

While the temple emitted a splendor all its own, its true brilliance came as it reflected the grandeur of its Creator. Surrounding the temple at equal intervals were twelve columns, each carefully engraved with a different name used by the angels to magnify some aspect of the King's perfect nature. At each column's base was a fountain filled to overflowing with a liquified form of Yahweh's glory. To the angels gazing up from below, it appeared like waterfalls of pure light cascading down the steep sides of the Holy Mount into reflection pools at its base.

Flowing from Yahweh's presence into the fifth heaven, indistinguishably united and yet somehow distinctly separate, was Ruach Elohim, the Holy Spirit of God. In what could best be described as a cloud, Ruach Elohim shielded the rest of the heavens from the glory of Yahweh. It was a sight so bright that the six-winged Seraphim were forced to use two of their wings to cover their eyes. Without Ruach Elohim's veil of protection, every angel in the four remaining heavens would be driven prostrate to the ground, seeking relief from the brilliance of the King.

The Mount of the Assembly stood in the recesses of the north in the fourth heaven, the second highest point in the kingdom of Elohim. Showered continually by the remnants of the fiery stones which marked Yahweh's footsteps around the temple, the Mount of the Assembly constantly shimmered like a burning torch. At its apex stood the Assembly Chamber, from which Yeshua governed all activities carried out by the heavenly host. As He sat on His elevated throne overlooking the Great Hall, the presence of Ruach Elohim flowed from above and encircled Yeshua in a unifying embrace. Outside, streets of gold, like rays of light from a star, radiated out in twelve directions from the Mount of the Assembly. Lining these streets were the main offices of the various Angelic Departments of Service. Combined, they were called Kavod Adonai, meaning "Glorify God."

The higher one went within Elohim's kingdom, the more energy and glory dominated the makeup of objects and surfaces rather than their physical presence. In the third level of heaven, the ground was covered with a soft, viscous substance called firmament. As one took a step in it, the firmament would mold around your foot, then ripple out like water circles flowing away from a stone cast in the Sea of Tranquility. With so many angels walking on the firmament, the ground in the higher levels of heaven constantly had the appearance of a flowing stream despite being solid in nature. This effect was most pronounced when viewed from below in the skies above the great gardens of God in the second heaven. Here, looking up, the sky appeared blue and looked like the rolling waves of an ocean.

Streets of gold carved roads through the firmament in the third level of heaven, with the satellite offices of the different angelic departments of service as well as various points of trade and community fellowship lining these roads as well. Beneath that, in the second level of heaven, were the residences of the angels. Here, the sky bore a unique, rose-colored hue, and the ground cover glowed in iridescent blues and greens. Yet, the texture of the ground was quite different than that found in the gardens of the first heaven.

In the first level of heaven, created by the King for the enjoyment of all who served Him, were the great gardens of God. While all were beautiful in their own way, every angel agreed, it was the garden called Eden which was the King's greatest artistic achievement. While a wide variety of vegetation and celestial wildlife were abundant throughout the kingdom, none could match that found in the Garden of Eden.

From the sixth level of heaven to the first level, all nine classes, or choirs, of the angelic host perpetually raised jubilant chants of praise to their King and Creator. Divided into three groups of three, called spheres, each class of angels filled a different capacity in the worship and service offered to the King. In the first sphere were angels known as the Seraphim, the Cherubim and the Thrones. Below them in the second sphere were the Dominions (also known as Lordships), the Virtues (or Strongholds), and the Powers (also called Authorities). Finally, in the third sphere, were the Principalities (or Rulers), the Archangels, and the subordinate Angels. Up and down the six levels of Heaven and among each of the nine classes of angels could be heard one phrase more than any other… "Blessed beyond measure."

******

Malachi often wondered why Lucifer continued to insist that they rendezvous at the same, small cabin on the backside of Eden, instead of at his spacious office in the center of the garden.

After all, the grating sounds made by the creaking doors and floors had intensified during their weeks together. Yet, once again, Malachi found himself standing on the same dilapidated porch, reaching for a doorknob on which was beginning to grow some type of black fungus. The whole scene sent a strange sensation up his spine. He shook his head and whispered, "This is Elohim's perfect kingdom? I must be missing something."

He turned the doorknob, expecting to hear the familiar high-pitched creak. Instead, the knob made no sound, not even a squeak. Relieved, he stepped into the cabin only to have his hopes dashed.

"Ah, there it is," he said, peering down at the wood slat beneath his foot which creaked as if objecting to being stepped on.

"There's what?" asked Lucifer from behind him. Malachi jumped. "Where did

The 9 Choirs of Angels	
1st Triad or Sphere	**Contemplate and Adore God Directly**
Seraphim	Name means the "burning ones." Attendants at the throne of God. Offer continuous praise to God saying, "Holy, Holy, Holy is the Lord God, Almighty."
Cherubim	Name means the "fullness of wisdom." Contemplate God's providence. Assigned to protect special places.
Thrones	Represent the steadfastness of the love of God. Contemplate God's power and judgment. Unlike others when revealed.
2nd Triad or Sphere	**Fulfill God's Plan in the Universe**
Dominions	Lord over the lower choirs and humanity. Take illumination from the higher hierarchies and govern the universe.
Virtues	Run the operation of movement in the universe. Often associated with planets, elements, season, and nature.
Powers	Assist in governing the natural order. Warrior angels tasked with fighting the war against the demonic choirs.
3rd Triad or Sphere	**Interact & Serve Humanity Closely**
Principalities	Princes of the lowest triad assigned to care for and guard communities, kingdoms, states, and parishes. Associated with transitions in power.
Archangels	Leader angels assigned to communicate and carry out God's important plans for man.
Angels	Closest to the material world and humanity. The lowest choir is where we get the majority of our personal guardian angels.

you come from?"

"I had another meeting that ran long. Decided to spirit-leap to try to beat you here."

The two angels chuckled as they made their way inside. Each step produced more of the same irritating sounds which accompanied all their visits together. Even the chairs creaked when the angels sat down.

Lucifer said, "That irritating noise keeps getting worse. I wish I knew what was causing it."

Malachi joked, "Maybe it's something you did."

"*What* is that supposed to mean?"

Lucifer's voice struck Malachi so powerfully that the young angel nearly fell out of his chair. It was a harsh reply unlike anything he'd ever heard before. Malachi didn't know how to react, so he tried to redirect the conversation.

"All this time, we've talked about the nature of Elohim and how to serve Him more effectively. I can't help but feel there must be something else you want to teach me?"

Lucifer's expression softened. "Do you remember what I said I would try to teach you when we first met?"

"How to faithfully serve our King."

"Yes, but can you remember anything else?"

"I think you mentioned something about reaching my full potential." "Yes, and I said you owed it to yourself to do so. Remember?"

"I don't really remember those words exactly, but ..."

"What I said was that you owe it to yourself to learn this—*Self* being the most important part of that statement."

"Self," said Malachi, "I don't understand that word. What does it mean?"

Lucifer stood. "Come with me. I have something to show you." He led Malachi to a small adjoining room for the first time since they began meeting together. Malachi had always assumed the room was of no importance, perhaps a closet. He was surprised to find the room completely empty except for a single chair, so ornate and enormous, it might better be described as a throne. While Malachi stood at the doorway, trying to make sense of what he saw, Lucifer walked over and sat down with his right leg draped over the chair's arm. He looked at Malachi and grinned. "What do you think?"

Malachi was uncertain how to answer. "Well ... it's beautiful. What is it doing out here in this rundown building?"

"It's for my eyes only; well, and now yours. Someday, the host of heaven can admire it."

"I'm not sure I understand. Why do you need such a throne?"

Rolling his eyes, Lucifer jumped up, grabbed Malachi by the arm and forced him to take a seat. "Now, tell me how you feel."

"A bit awkward."

"What do you mean, *awkward*?"

"It seems like the kind of chair only a king would use, and I'm certainly not a king. Only Elohim is worthy to sit upon such a finely crafted throne. Only He is King."

Lucifer turned away, concealing the expression on his face, and mumbled something under his breath.

"I'm sorry, Lucifer. I didn't quite hear that."

His mentor jerked around and growled, "Isn't it possible the angel that Elohim described as 'the One' should have a throne like this?"

The whole conversation seemed inappropriate for one created to glorify Elohim. Malachi quickly stood and made for the exit. As he entered the main room, he called over his shoulder, "If this is what you mean by *Self*, I want no part of it." He turned towards the front door. When he did, he found himself face-to-face with Lucifer, who had spirit-leaped between him and the exit.

Lucifer said, "You don't even know who you are. The King says you're 'the One,' and you don't even ask why He made that distinction. Is it not possible Elohim views you as something far more important than any of the rest of His heavenly host? For all you know, He asked me to make this chair for you. Instead, you don't even seek to know your true identity. You don't even seek to know why He created you."

Malachi stopped. He'd never considered that there might be something special about himself. But, Lucifer's words seemed to carry an element of truth. Was he disregarding Elohim's word in the weight of humility?

After all, Elohim did endorse all mentorship assignments. If there was a problem with this one, He would never have confirmed it.

"I'm sorry, Sir. It just sounds strange to think the King would create me to be unique from the rest of the heavenly host."

"Well, open your eyes," Lucifer snapped. "You aren't the only angel He created that way."

"What do you mean?" asked Malachi.

"What do you think I am? Don't answer. I'll tell you." Lucifer walked back to the table and chairs they'd been using the past several weeks. He extended his hand and invited Malachi to take a seat. Hesitantly, Malachi obliged.

Lucifer began, "Why do you think Elohim created any of us?"

"To give Him praise and worship."

"Yes, but He doesn't need your praise and worship. He's perfect. So, why did He really create all of us?"

Malachi could only sit in silence. Exasperated, he finally responded, "I don't know. If He doesn't need our praise, why do you think He did it?"

"Elohim may not need anything. But, a need and a want are two entirely different things. Our praise is not an end in itself."

"What could Elohim possibly want that He doesn't already have? He's perfect and complete. Maybe He just wanted to grant someone else the greatest gift they could ever receive—the opportunity to praise and worship Him. I know I feel blessed beyond measure to have the chance to worship the glorious God who created me...to actually have a relationship with Him."

Lucifer tapped his temple and let out a chuckle. Gesturing at Malachi in a way that seemed half pointing, half taunting, he said, "That's getting closer. Maybe there is hope for you yet."

Bewildered, Malachi ran his hands across his bald head, searching for the answer. Aware of the puzzled expression on his protégé's face, Lucifer said, "You still don't understand."

Malachi replied, "OK, so in your opinion, why did Elohim create us to freely praise Him?"

******

"But Thou art holy, O Thou that inhabitest the praises of Israel."

Psalm 22:3

******

Lucifer placed a hand on Malachi's shoulder and answered, "As I said, our praise is not an end in and of itself. The value of praise comes in its ability to create a space not otherwise in existence that our King, both as One Essence and Three Personages, is able to inhabit."

"I'm not sure why that would compel Elohim to create all of us. He's omnipresent already. Why would He need to exist anywhere else?"

Lucifer shook his head and replied, "So, let's see if you can figure it out on your own. Here's a clue...you mentioned it earlier. What is the greatest treasure anyone can find if Elohim really is all He presents Himself to be?"

"Well, I would say the greatest treasure would be to find Him and to have a relationship with Him," answered Malachi.

"Right. So, if more of Elohim is the greatest treasure for one such as you and me, could it not also be true for our King? Would He not be driven by an internal want for more of Himself if such was a possibility?"

Malachi shook his head and said, "It's too hard to understand."

"Of course it is. Elohim is higher than all of our thoughts regarding Him. Most find it impossible to comprehend our One God having a triune existence. I'm asking you to think a step further...something even more complex. I'm asking you to consider the ramifications of His triune existence."

Lucifer leaned across the table, pressing his fingers into the wood as if trying to make his point directly to it. He explained, "It is within our praise that the three Personages of our King can find an otherwise non-existent place in which They have a common presence. In fact, it is within that freely offered praise that the Trinity finds its deepest intimacy with each other. It is that desire for greater intimacy between the three Personages of the Trinity that compelled our King to create us with free will."

Malachi now shook his head, this time not in disagreement. He shook it in disbelief. "That makes sense. He's one in Essence, so Elohim wouldn't need anything else to make Him more complete; however, the distinct Personages of the Trinity might find greater intimacy between Them within our praise. That internal want might compel Him to create all of us to praise and worship Him."

After a few moments of silent reflection, Malachi continued, "So, if that's why you believe He made all of us, what is the special reason He created you?"

A strange look rushed across Lucifer's face—like confidence, but unlike any Malachi had ever seen. Lucifer wasn't displaying confidence in Elohim. It was in...himself.

Lucifer said, "Blessed beyond measure. Blessed beyond measure. You do understand how that works, don't you?"

"It's our greeting to one another, but it's also a word of praise to our King."

"That's almost correct." Lucifer paced in front of the table. "But there's much more to that as well. You see, the rhythmic sound of the words when spoken within any one of the six levels of Elohim's heavenly kingdom sound more like a chant than a song when the King hears them. Combine them together as one though, and the result is a harmonic tone the beauty of which is beyond the limits of imagination."

"But, Elohim's creativity has no limits."

Lucifer grinned as he walked over to Malachi, placed a hand on his shoulder, and leaned close to his ear. "And, that's part of what makes *me* a special creation. You see, Elohim knew there was a tone upon which all the rest could be grounded; one which would make the combined sound richer and the praise to Him even greater. In His wisdom, Elohim recognized that sound would need to be raised by a single voice, one stronger and more beautiful than all the rest. After all, there can be innumerable harmonies, but only one melody. So, in the fullness of time, Elohim created a voice which could carry the melody in *Blessed beyond measure*. At just the right moment in eternity, Elohim created…me."

Lucifer smirked as he patted himself on the chest. "It is my voice which provides the glorious melody when we say *Blessed beyond measure*. It is my voice that completes the praise we offer up to Elohim and in which Yahweh, Yeshua, and Ruach Elohim find the depth of intimacy they seek. Without *my* voice as the foundation, our praise for Elohim would be incomplete and imperfect. Without *me*, you and every other angel would no longer be able to live in the six levels of Elohim's heavenly kingdom. Your praise would be imperfect, and nothing imperfect can be in His presence."

Malachi found himself speechless. There was something not quite right about how the Angel of Light described his role in that act of praise. Somehow, it seemed more about himself than about Elohim.

Malachi's apprehension rose further as Lucifer said, "If our angelic praise given freely to Elohim is not perfect, then He would be left with something about Himself which is less than perfect, even if that imperfection were just to be the slightest bit discontent. Knowing there could be a deeper level of intimacy within Himself if only our praise was perfect would breed discontentment. And, at what point does discontentment become imperfection?"

"Don't you see? Everything hinges on me. God may be our Creator and Provider, but I am our Sustainer in many ways."

CHAPTER THREE

THE ANOINTED CHERUB WHO COVERS

"Why do you call Me, 'Lord, Lord,'

and not do what I say?"

Luke 6:46

Final Day of Malachi's Mentorship

Malachi turned the knob and opened the door to the rundown cabin for the last time. As usual, the air inside was filled with the sharp, creaking sound which had been a constant companion throughout his mentorship. Though he had given up trying to identify its source, he never stopped wondering why the noise only made an appearance when he was with Lucifer.

As he entered the cabin, the Angel of Light asked, "Any new ideas regarding why the King referred to you as 'the One?'"

Malachi laughed. "Not a clue. Perhaps I am the one whose purpose in existence will remain a mystery forever. Maybe we should just spend the day together enjoying each other's company. After all, it is our last time to meet as part of my mentorship."

Lucifer looked up from the pile of scrolls through which he'd been sorting.

Frustration—no anger—oozed from every inch of his countenance. He barked, "Glad you can find humor at a time like this. Today is our last chance to learn what the King meant. We can't stop until we figure it out."

"Why does it matter so much to you? Maybe it's something Elohim wants to reveal to me in the future. If He wills for me to know it now, then great. But what if He wants me to experience other events prior to showing me? Can't I just serve Him patiently until He reveals that truth to me?"

Lucifer crumpled a scroll and buried his head in it. Softly, and as if he was trying to measure his words through the flame of his emotions, he snarled, "Wait patiently for Elohim? We could be waiting forever. No, I deserve to know what He meant...now."

Somewhere in the depths of his innermost being, Malachi heard the soft prompting of Ruach Elohim. *Wait a second.* In a voice not quite his own, Malachi boldly challenged his mentor, "You deserve to know what He meant when He called *me* 'the One?' Why do you deserve to know something about me? I don't even know if I deserve to know it yet. What and when Elohim chooses to reveal is a matter of His will, and I will choose to be satisfied with whatever He decides. Anything else would be to put my will ahead of His own."

"And, what's so wrong with that?" Lucifer challenged. "It's your destiny, not His. You have a right to control anything that relates to your being."

Malachi couldn't believe how far Lucifer seemed to have slipped away from making Elohim's will the desire of his own heart. "Are you saying accomplishing your will is just as important as carrying out the King's will?"

"In some ways, yes," replied Lucifer. "I'm still working this out for myself. I do know that true fulfillment only comes when we are true to ourselves. If we always submit to the King's will in everything, even when we may want something different, is that what is best for us? Is that really what is best for the King? Think about it."

"Are you serious?" asked Malachi.

"Absolutely." Sincerity etched across his mentor's face. "After all, isn't perfection an absolute for our King? How can His kingdom still be perfect if those who serve Him are constantly placed in a state of discontentment? The perfection of paradise is not founded on the perspective of just one of its inhabitants...no matter who that One might be."

Malachi found himself torn. The angels' existence was not about Lucifer's will or any other angel's will. It was about carrying out their Creator's will. Still, how could perfection be maintained when Lucifer's will differed from God's?

What if my will becomes different from the King's? Perhaps Lucifer is right. Maybe the only way to maintain perfection is to find the way to serve both Elohim and ourselves. But, which comes first?

Malachi closed his eyes for a moment and prayed, *Elohim, I want to do what is right in Your sight. I know my greatest calling is to do Your will; however, I can see how choosing to not do my own would introduce imperfection into Your kingdom.*

Which is more important?

Ruach Elohim whispered His response into Malachi's spirit like a gentle breeze filtering through the leaves. *Seek first My kingdom and My righteousness, and all these things will be added unto you. Delight yourself in Me, and I will give you the desires of your heart.* The answer was clear: Do God's will first.

It seemed to Malachi that Lucifer was searching for a way to make "my will be done" possible without bringing himself into conflict with Elohim. It was also clear he still hadn't discovered the solution.

As they broke to go their separate ways, Malachi reflected back over the things he'd heard from Lucifer. Many lessons stood out regarding how to serve the King more effectively. Still, he wondered, *Did I learn more about serving our King, or about questioning the absolute preeminence of His will?*

Malachi's mentorship ended with the same pressing questions remaining as they had had on the first day. Neither he nor Lucifer knew why Malachi was "the One," and Lucifer still couldn't understand how he could pursue his own will over Elohim's without somehow being at odds with the King. Instead of a warm embrace and well-wishes for the future, Malachi left the cabin in silence, Lucifer's head buried in a scroll as his final image from the experience.

* * * * * *

Following his mentorship assignment with Lucifer, Malachi began his formal service of the King. In each assignment, he demonstrated unparalleled devotion to His Creator, both in his reverence for the King and zeal for his will. There was no thought of Self…only *Thy will be done, O Lord.*

But as eternity passed, Malachi began to wonder, *How much longer must I wait to learn what God meant when He called me 'the One'. What amazing work am I to perform on His behalf? What role am I to play?*

The more he thought about it, the more difficult it became to wait for Elohim's answer.

Perhaps Lucifer was right during my mentorship when he said, 'Wait patiently for Elohim? We could be waiting forever.' Surely, there is something I can do to get things moving. Maybe I am supposed to do something first. I can't just sit and wait on Elohim to act. It's my destiny, and it's the future He purposed for me. How could helping things along be wrong?" "I'll get permission to go visit Lucifer. Perhaps I can get assigned to him again. He's much closer to Elohim after all. Maybe if I am closer to the King, it will remind Him to act on His proclamation. Then finally, I can be "the One."*

CHAPTER FOUR

MY WILL BE DONE

"You were the anointed cherub who covers, and I placed you there. You were
on the holy mountain of God; you walked in the midst of the stones of fire."
Ezekiel 28:14

Eternity Past...after Lucifer's mentorship of Malachi

Lucifer looked out over Eden from his office in the middle of the vast garden. To the north, he watched as the great river, Sovereignty, branched out from the base of the Tree of Life to form four rivers which themselves split into numerous tributaries carrying water across the vast landscape. To the east, fields of wildflowers, some created by Elohim, others bred by Lucifer, waved like flags beneath the gentle breeze flowing down from the rocky cliffs in the west. It was here, dropping nearly 120 feet into the Pools of Serenity, that Forever Falls found its home.

Hundreds of thousands of angels visited Eden each day from their quarters in the second level of heaven, taking time to pray and worship their King in a setting which reminded all that He alone was God. For most angels, it was another opportunity to bring the King greater glory. The Angel of Light, however, now reached an entirely different conclusion. As he observed the reaction inspired by 'his' garden and 'his' music, a subtle thought crept into his mind. *I wonder if anyone else recognizes how greatly my works honor Elohim?*

* * * * * *

Though imperceptible to the other angels, Elohim, the Omniscient Creator of all, recognized the danger contained in Lucifer's seemingly innocent question. To a perfect God, there was nothing subtle about his statement. It was a paradigm shift in thinking. The roots of self, previously firmly established in Lucifer's head, had now made their way to his heart. Passionate service of the King for His glory and for the fulfillment of His will now gave way to a desire for recognition for himself in those efforts. Elohim understood the significance of that shift.

Immediately, a divine counsel of the triune Personages of the Godhead convened in the Holy of Holies.

The first to enter was Ruach Elohim, His presence in the form of a cloud dispersing throughout the chamber before engulfing the golden lamp stand to the left of Yahweh's throne. As soon as He settled on the beautiful fixture, its seven candles ignited, adding their brilliant light to the ever-present glory of Yahweh throughout the room.

Next, Yeshua stepped into the chamber and moved to the right of Yaweh's throne. Yeshua placed His hand on the shoulder of a Seraphim who was positioned next to the Altar of Incense. The Seraphim lit the altar, and a pleasing aroma wafted upward, filling the Holy of Holies with its soothing fragrance.

Finally, the fullness of Yahweh's radiance filled the chamber, bathing all in His glory. As was customary, Yeshua lifted up a prayer on behalf of those He always referred to as "His beloved" or "His future saints." He prayed for their faithfulness, for their repentance, for their salvation and growth. He prayed that they would be in the world which was to come, but not of that world. He prayed they would not be tricked into believing a lie by the one who would levy accusations against Him in the future. And, He prayed that all would freely choose dependence upon Him rather than independence from Him.

No angel completely understood the nature of the prayer; however, speculation was that Yeshua prayed for a being yet to be created. While the timing of that being's beginning remained a mystery, there was no doubt it would be of utmost importance in the future.

As soon as Yeshua and Ruach Elohim finished, Yahweh declared, "All has transpired as We knew it would. Within the praise of the angels, We found a space We could inhabit wherein We could enjoy a depth of intimacy that was impossible without the heavenly host."

Yeshua added, "Yes, but as We knew, such space can only be found within volitional praise, and that only comes where a relationship exists. For there to be true relationship, both parties must have free will."

Ruach Elohim said, "But where there is free will, there is always a risk. It holds the only power capable of threatening Our perfection. For within free will, lies the capacity to choose *Self* above Our perfect will."

"Our quandary was twofold," continued Yahweh. "Create the angels with free will and receive the benefits of their volitional praise while knowing much pain and suffering will come their way, or don't create the angels and face what comes to Us with unrighteous discontentment. Choose the latter, and We face an eternity of imperfect existence."

"We face Our own personal Hell," said Ruach Elohim.

"Choose the former, and a period of calamity and chaos will arise," said Yeshua as He rubbed His wrists, a pained expression rushing across His face.

"That's the heart of our quandary. We know eventually Lucifer and many others will choose Selfish ambitions over devotion to Our will. It's why We chose to not create the angels for as long as We did. After all, we don't need the praise and worship of anything to be anymore content within Ourselves than We are. We are One. Yet, We are Three. Is there anyone, including Ourselves, who, if they were able to be more intimately close to Us, would not become discontent if that opportunity was withheld from them? The answer to that We know is…no."

"Of course," Yeshua said, "and that's why Our dilemma is so complicated. It isn't just about their eternal destiny. It's about Ours. For Us to choose not to fulfill this want is to threaten Our own eternity with a living Hell. At some point, that unfulfilled Want turns to Discontentment, and Discontentment ushers in Imperfection."

Yahweh said, "We have to act. Imperfection is not an option for Us. Though living forever, We would eternally die."

Ruach Elohim said, "Our eyes are too pure to behold iniquity. Nothing imperfect can be in Our presence. That which is perfect is wholly incompatible with the imperfect."

"But now, Lucifer has started down that imperfect path of Self. Despite his wisdom, he's not even aware of the difference embodied in seeking recognition from others, but it is tremendous," added Yeshua. "Seeking recognition for his efforts means trying to glorify himself, even if only in the smallest of ways."

"And, that idea will grow and spread from there," said Yahweh.

Ruach Elohim warned, "Before long, that need for recognition will consume him. Eventually, it will become his greatest desire. Once it does, recognition won't be the only thing he's after. Recognition seeks glory. Glory seeks its will over

Our will. And that focus on Self eventually leads to seeking sovereignty—Our sovereignty."

"Our dilemma remains," said Yeshua. "Do nothing and imperfection takes hold. Prevent any of them from going down the path of Self, and We take away their free will. To do that is to destroy true relationship, volitional praise, and Our access to greater intimacy between Us."

"And that leads Us back to discontentment and imperfection," said Yahweh. "Let Us devise a plan which preserves Our perfection, offers free will to all, and preserves as many as We can within the framework of free will. It will be a balancing act that will require perfect timing for every move We make. Our perfection will be maintained in Our ability to sustain a perfect balance between achievement of Our will and preservation of their free will. Ultimately, We must return all to Our perfect and pleasing will."

"So, what can we offer Lucifer as a way of escape?" asked Yeshua. "Somehow, it must be handled in a manner which preserves his free will."

"Free will is a tricky force to steer," said Yahweh. "Direct it too much, and it is destroyed altogether. Direct it too little, and Our kingdom is threatened."

All were silent.

A moment later, Yeshua suggested, "Perhaps if We were the One to shower him with recognition, Lucifer would change his course voluntarily?" No sooner had He said the words did He counter, "No, it doesn't make a difference in his future. Lucifer's heart will harden."

"Yes. That is what I see as well," said Ruach Elohim. "Yet, We must grant him the opportunity to choose a different path. It must be granted to all of them. If not, We will have chosen their course for them. Instead of a relationship with Lucifer or any other angel, We will have orchestrated little more than divine puppetry, and that would bring about the end of all praise. That would bring about the end of Our perfection and usher Us into Our own Hell."

Yahweh said, "Let it be so. Shower him with the recognition he seeks. We will have given him the chance to soften, given him a chance to bathe his heart in a spirit of gratitude rather than Selfish ambition. Perhaps it will drown out this yearning for 'My will be done,' and restore his desire for Our perfect will."

Yeshua added, "And, may it happen before those roots burrow so deeply into his heart that he cannot return to us or that they branch out and infest the hearts of others among the heavenly host."

Elohim set His eternal plan into motion beginning with recognizing Lucifer. From that moment on, no other angels received the breadth and depth of recognition offered to Lucifer. Only time would tell if Elohim, through His omnipotence, could alter a destiny He knew to be beyond correction.

* * * * * *

No one was surprised when Elohim once again promoted Lucifer to an even greater position.

It seemed fitting given the bounty of jewels and gems already awarded to him as medals for his outstanding performance. While Overseer of the Garden of Eden was certainly a prominent assignment, Elohim saw fit to anoint and ordain Lucifer as a Cherub and to make him Primicerius, the highest ranking official at the Department of Worship. Elohim withheld nothing from Lucifer, even allowing him to walk in His very presence on the Holy Mount, where fiery stones marked each of the King's steps. While the move surprised no one, none of the angels were aware of Elohim's true motives.

* * * * * *

As eternity rolled on, Lucifer's *need to be recognized* as Elohim's greatest servant continued to grow and became the primary motivation behind his acts of service. Eventually, that fixation found a focus in the idea he first contemplated in the Garden of Eden and which he cultivated during his time on the Holy Mount. Rather than a life purposed towards glorifying and serving Elohim, his existence now focused on Self. Self-*centeredness*. Self-*absorption*. Self-*satisfaction*. Self-*gratification*. Selfish *ambition*. The more he meditated on the concept, the more the roots burrowed into his heart. Finally, Lucifer was so immersed in Self that he could think of almost nothing else. Serving Elohim was now secondary to the pursuit of his new god. Lucifer went so far as to commission statues of himself to be made from the best sculptors and placed throughout the Garden. In the Department of Worship, new stained-glass windows depicted Lucifer as an angel above all others. In some quarters, murals of his face began to appear on the sides of buildings.

Despite Elohim's best efforts to fulfill Lucifer's desire for recognition, He could clearly see the outcome. Yahweh said to Yeshua and Ruach Elohim, "We've done all We can do in this first stage of Our plan. It's time to move to the next stage, even if it costs Us all that We have enjoyed. It is time to make 'the announcement.'"

CHAPTER FIVE

EVERY GOOD GIFT

"Every good thing given and every perfect gift is from above, coming down from the father of lights, with whom there is no variation or shifting shadow."

James 1:17

Malachi's nerves felt on edge as he sat and waited his turn to speak with his former mentor and, at least he hoped, friend. It was an odd sensation, certainly uncommon among angels, and yet, the queasy feeling in his stomach was undeniable. Angels filled the waiting area outside the Primicerius' door. Another line of them continued into the streets outside the Department of Worship's main office in the fourth heaven.

I wonder how many of these angels are waiting to speak with Lucifer, just hoping for a chance to work here. As Malachi locked eyes with another angel, he whispered to himself, "Is this really going to make any difference?" It seemed like such a long shot. *What if he doesn't remember me? It's been so long since we last spoke. What if I didn't even make a good impression on him when he was my mentor? After all, we left each other's company on such odd terms in the end.* The more he thought, the more his stomach churned.

Finally, he started to gather his things so he could make a hasty exit. However, before he could get to his feet, a Department of Worship aide called from the doorway leading to the back offices, "Malachi, Department of Celestial Fellowship."

"Too late," he muttered to himself. He stood and followed the aide down a long hallway towards what Malachi anticipated might be an embarrassing moment for either his former mentor or himself. Beneath his feet was a checkerboard of polished gray and white granite. At equal intervals lining the walls, golden columns rose from the floor like the stately oaks of Meditation Forest in the Third Heaven.

As the columns reached the ceiling, they spread apart to form a canopy of thinly cut emerald and lapis lazuli gems shaped like leaves. In between each column, stained-glass windows depicted scenes typically found in each of the six levels of Elohim's Kingdom.

As Malachi walked past each window, what was depicted came alive, visually transporting him to that level of heaven for just a moment. So intricate were the scenes presented in the stained glass that they captured even the cascading nature in which the levels of heaven overlapped with one another, the spiritual realm of the lower serving as the physical realm of the higher. Oddly enough, it seemed Lucifer could be found in each window, growing successively in prominence. At the last window, Malachi stopped to study the beautiful image more closely. As the image moved towards its final form, a scene of worship at the Holy Mount came to view. Millions of angels ascended gold steps, switching back-and-forth on their way to the summit.

When they arrived, all fell to their knees, giving worship to— Malachi's attention was suddenly drawn elsewhere.

At the end of the hallway stood a large set of double doors. Each door was twelve feet tall and five feet wide, made from white pearl so pure in quality that Malachi could see himself in its reflection. Written in liquefied silver on a black onyx plate beside the door was:

LUCIFER
PRIMICERIUS: DEPARTMENT OF WORSHIP
"ANGEL OF LIGHT" / CHERUB

The aide escorted Malachi into the office of the most famous of all the heavenly host. "Please, take a seat. The Primicerius will be with you shortly."

For several minutes, Malachi waited for Lucifer to make his appearance. When it became apparent his delay would be significant, Malachi worked up the courage to stand and look at the beautiful accommodations in which he now found himself.

Located throughout the room were items made in each of the six levels of heaven. Beautiful artwork created using materials from the first level of heaven were displayed in every imaginable medium on Lucifer's walls. Ornate pottery and sculptures from the Second Heaven were displayed on every flat surface. Malachi's eyes were especially drawn to the goblets and a carafe made from the iron-rich clays found along the banks of the Sea of Tranquility; the clay being inlaid with gold from the sea's feeder rivers, each set in a uniquely intricate design. So pure was the craftsmanship that when Malachi ran his fingers across the carafe, he could distinguish no seams where the gold and clay met. Finally, Malachi found himself standing in front of the central feature of the office, the Angel of Light's desk and the throne-like chair Malachi had seen back in the cabin during his mentorship with Lucifer.

Without warning, a voice broke the silence behind him, "The desk is made from wood I selected out of my garden in the first heaven. Designed it myself."

Malachi jumped as his old mentor burst through a side doorway. Lucifer continued, "Interestingly, while I love the richness found in its dark grain, it was actually the smell of the wood which originally drew me. The musk of pine and the sweetness of the honeydew tree. My chair, of course, you have seen before."

Just as Malachi started to answer, Lucifer held up a palm. "Hold on another minute. I'm almost finished with my earlier meeting. Take a seat, and I'll be back." In an existence set within eternity, did a delay of any length really matter?

Lucifer left before Malachi could respond. He sighed and whispered, "I can't believe he caught me wandering around his office looking at his things. How presumptuous he must think I am!"

Looking through one of the office windows, Malachi watched as Lucifer walked out onto a patio in the western tower. He engaged with three other angels in what appeared to be a serious discussion. Malachi wondered about the kind of angels Lucifer must consistently entertain and what important subjects they must cover. He sat down in the chair from which he had begun his ill-advised tour of the office.

Finally, the discussion broke up and the small group of angels headed towards the door. As they entered the office and crossed its expanse, one angel looked back and said in a loud voice, "We'll do our best, Sir. I'm certain they'll see the wisdom in your ideas. We'll especially target…"

Lucifer interrupted the angel, "As you can see, my next guest has arrived. I will speak with the King about what we discussed as soon as my schedule permits."

The trio of angels shot strange glances at Malachi, then left the room.

"Malachi, my old friend, I'm so glad you came." Lucifer's eyes beamed with a smile, as the Angel of Light took a seat behind his desk. "I've wanted to see you for so long. Not sure why, but I was only just recently granted permission to pull you away from your work to…where is it that you are working now?"

"The Department of Celes—"

"Oh yes, important work. Hold on for just a second."

An aide stepped forward, his arms piled high with parchments, all of which seemed to require Lucifer's signature.

As Malachi waited, he looked around the room trying to appear unaffected by this intrusion on their time together. He noticed a painting of the Garden of Eden on a golden easel just behind the Primicerius' desk. In the bottom corner of the painting was the unmistakable signature of Lucifer.

"Beautiful artwork," Malachi commented when Lucifer's attention returned to him.

Lucifer rose from his chair and stood beside the painting. "Thanks for noticing. Most of my spare time is spent in my music, but I love art as well, and I especially love works related to my garden. Anyway, I'm glad you were able to come spend some time with me."

"You might be wondering what I was discussing with that group of angels. It's a furtherance of the idea of Self I've been contemplating increasingly since we met together during your mentorship period. At this point, I feel that message is finally ready to be shared with others. I've worked out a lot of the rough edges you and I seemed to be at odds over the last time we spoke. I believe now every angel will be able to agree with and support the concept of Self and all it represents."

"Really?"

"Yes, really."

"Well, then, how can I help in getting the word out?"

For the first time since Malachi arrived in his office, Lucifer appeared interested in what his former protégé had to say. Lucifer tilted his head with a raised eyebrow. "What is it you said you do now?"

"I'm an associate at the Department of Celestial Fellowship," answered Malachi, stunned at having to repeat himself given how quickly Lucifer had dismissed his previous attempt to share the same.

"And, how do you think that could be helpful?"

Before Malachi had a chance to answer, another knock came to Lucifer's door.

"Hold on for just a second more." Lucifer stood and moved just beyond Malachi's view to a door leading presumably to the offices of his staff. Malachi was unable to hear what was being said. From Lucifer's expression, something urgent was being brought to his attention.

When he returned, Lucifer said, "Malachi, I will have to cut our meeting short today. Is there anything I can specifically do for you?"

"Well, I have always wanted to be back under your tutelage. I know every angel in the heavens would like to work in the Department of Worship, but I was hoping you might have an opening on your staff for which I could interview."

The Primicerius scanned a list on his desk. "As it turns out, we do have at least one open associate position, so here is what I will do. These positions are highly sought after, so I can't promise anything. However, I will have my Director of Operations, Adramelech, take a look at your credentials and get in touch with you if he thinks there is any possibility you might meet the job description. If it goes well, who knows?"

Without even pausing to hear Malachi's response, Lucifer set off to his next appointment. Struggling to hide his disappointment, Malachi thought, *Well, I'm sure Lucifer makes offers of this kind all the time. I won't get my hopes up.*

* * * * * *

Malachi arrived at the Department of Celestial Fellowship, sat down at his workstation, and buried his face in his hands. His expectations had been so high when he lined up the meeting with his old mentor. In his mind, he always pictured a warm embrace, an exchange of fond memories, inspirational words and then some type of support in obtaining a position in the Department of Worship.

Now his mind raced. *I guess that was just a dream.*

Lost in his thoughts, Malachi completely missed the arrival of his departmental supervisor. Barnabas, one of the first angels created by the King, looked unlike any other angel. A scraggly, white beard, drooping brow line, and pale, wrinkled skin made some question the eternality of angels. However, there was a different story behind his frail appearance; a strength and dedication Malachi respected immensely. Barnabas had actually requested that his stature and appearance be old and weak. When other angels questioned the wisdom in his request, Barnabas simply replied, "Your physical stature may demonstrate well the creative capacity of our King, but my frailty brings Him glory of an entirely different nature. Don't you see? His omnipotence is made more apparent each time He accomplishes something through me despite my weakness."

Now, standing at the entryway to Malachi's workstation, Barnabas asked, "Well, son, how did your visit go?"

"Nothing close to what I hoped."

"Why? What happened?"

"I should have known what was coming as soon as I had to wait so long in Lucifer's lobby. Sure, he said he was glad to see me, but how sincere was that?" Malachi proceeded to share each wrenching detail of his appointment with Lucifer. When he finished, he was stunned by Barnabas' silence and incredulous expression.

"Sir, did you hear me? You'd be disappointed, too, had you been in a similar position. Wouldn't you?' asked Malachi.

Again, only silence.

"Seriously, Sir. For all my effort, I just got passed off to a subordinate. Now would be a good time to live up to your name. I need some encouragement."

Barnabas answered, "Oh really? Because it doesn't sound like you're looking for encouragement at all. Sounds like you think a different position is the only thing that will make things right. Encouragement...here's my word of encouragement for you. In the past, you've told me you want more than anything else to serve Elohim wherever He sees fit to place you. Is that still right?"

"Of course, Barnabas. You know that's how I feel."

"So, if Elohim continues to have you work in the Department of Celestial Fellowship, what do you care? You're exactly where He wants you to serve Him right now. Oh, and if He decides He really wants you to work for Him out of the Department of Worship, don't you believe Elohim would get the Angel of Light to act on that desire?"

"Well, sure, but Elohim knows my motivation. Why would Elohim say 'no?'"

As he always did when contemplating a question, Barnabas began scratching behind his right ear with his left hand. "Sure, He knows what motivates every angel's heart. So, think about it; why would He possibly say 'no?'"

Now it was Malachi's turn to scratch his head. He had to admit, he couldn't think of a good answer. Finally, a thought entered his mind... "The King always says, 'Delight yourself in Me, and I will give you the desires of your heart.'"

"I've always seen that to be the case. I would encourage..." Barnabas smiled and winked at Malachi, setting off a moment of levity. "I would encourage you to ask Elohim. He's always open to such discussions. However, if He lingers in His response to you, recognize He's either saying 'not now' or He's about to start changing the desires of your heart to match those of His own."

"I'll get to work on a message to Elohim immediately," said Malachi.

"Umm...well, how about you do some work for me first. Your all-day meeting with Lucifer has our team behind now. We may be just the Department of Celestial Fellowship, but I'm pretty fond of it. Oh, and the King seems to think what we do is pretty important as well." Barnabas pulled a golden envelope from his satchel.

"Is that from the office of the King?" Malachi asked.

"Well, let me see." Barnabas pulled a thick, golden card from the envelope. "Yes, it does seem to carry the seal of the King, and it does come from the office of Elohim's Chief of Staff." He handed the card to Malachi.

A mixture of surprise and excitement danced across Malachi's face. "An invitation to attend a special announcement tomorrow in the Great Hall on the Mount of the Assembly? That means being in the presence of Yeshua before His throne. This is incredible. You must be so excited to go."

"Who said I was going?" answered Barnabas.

"If not you, then who?"

Barnabas smiled. "Check the envelope again."

Malachi reached inside and found another message on the Chief of Staff's letterhead. In addition to praising the efforts of every angel under Barnabas's supervision, the note explicitly asked that Malachi be sent as the department's representative to the meeting. He couldn't believe what he was reading.

Barnabas shook his head, grinning. "I guess that's two days' worth of work you're going to owe me now."

CHAPTER SIX

SWORDPLAY

*"For he is the minister of God to thee for good. But if thou do that
which is evil, be afraid; for He beareth not the sword in vain: for he is the
minister of God, a revenger to [execute] wrath upon him that doeth evil."*

Romans 13:4

L ucifer arrived at the Mount of the Assembly early that day following
receipt of his own golden invitation to appear at the King's announcement
event. His step was purposeful, light, and almost gleeful as he strode
along the golden streets of the city known among the angels as simply
"His Presence." While he didn't like to be pulled away from his duties on either the
Holy Mount or at the Department of Worship, he could tell from the nature of the
invitation that Elohim had something important to present to his leading angels.
Lucifer felt certain there could be but one announcement which would require
their immediate presence in the Assembly.

The entire way he thought, *Today, I finally get what is rightfully mine. No longer
will I continue as just one among many Cherubim. Though I have been greater
than every other angel in the heavenly host for many millennia, it's finally time
my public rank reflected that superior state. Once I am officially recognized as the
greatest of the stars of heaven, surely Elohim will create a new rank for me alone, a
new sphere in which I am the only member.*

There is no angel to whom I should answer regardless of rank. He quietly
whispered, "Today is the day. I will raise my throne above the stars of God." This
was more than a metaphor. Lucifer truly saw the chair he'd fashioned for himself
during his days as Overseer of the Garden of Eden as his own personal throne.
Now, it sat waiting in his office in the Third Heaven for the day when the Garden's

former Overseer would be viewed as the recognized leader of all the heavenly host.

Even though he had been promoted to the Holy Mount where he was among a select few angels driving the worship of the King in His very presence, Lucifer's heart in many ways remained in "his" garden. More specifically, his desires were immersed in his ambition to reign over every angel in the heavens. Anticipating this end, Lucifer was already secretly forming a core group of angels around himself who embraced the glory of *Self*. These angels, the Watchers, even now followed the Angel of Light's lead almost as dutifully as Elohim's. Watching and waiting... anticipating the day when they would be ordered into action.

Walking up the steps of the Mount of the Assembly and looking about him in this fourth level of the current heavens, Lucifer marveled to himself, *Of all things beautiful here in the heavens, is there anything more beautiful than I? Is there really anything here or on the Holy Mount, which is more spectacular than what I made in the Garden of Eden? Surely all can see that what my hands fashion is as wonderful as what Elohim creates. Even Elohim will have to admit it and reward me in accordance with that greatness.*

He had been trying to think of what reward was fitting for one as accomplished as himself. As he neared the Assembly Chamber, the answer came to him with perfect clarity. "I will sit on the Mount of the Assembly in the recesses of the north. I will place my throne on Yahweh's left. With Yeshua seated on Yahweh's right, together we will rule over all. I will be recognized as an equal and my fame will be beyond comparison with any other created being."

* * * * * *

It never gets old, thought Malachi as he gazed into the skies overlooking the third heaven. Golden streams of reflected light flowed upwards before disappearing as millions of angels made their way through the transheaven portals separating the third and fourth heavens.

Usually movement through the portals was sporadic, but this was not a normal occasion. Malachi reached into his satchel and ran his fingers over the invitation to the King's announcement event.

He shrugged his shoulders and shook his head. Moments later, he joined the line of angels waiting their turn.

Certainly, spirit leaping was a faster way to make the ascent, but Malachi wanted to cherish every moment of this special blessing. The energy among the angels in line was thrilling. None knew what the announcement would be, but many had their ideas. He paused for a moment just to listen to some of the other guests making their way to the Assembly Chamber. As he listened, most assumed the announcement centered around angelic leadership promotions. He overheard the angels in one group saying: "After all, why would the King ask all department leaders to attend unless it involved promotions at our level?"

"I agree, but there has to be more to it than that. I think it must involve Lucifer. He's done so much of late. Surely he is being recognized once again."

"I heard Elohim is creating a new level within the Angelic Hierarchy; one which sets him alone above all others."

Malachi suddenly felt a hand on his shoulder. When he spun around, he was surprised to be looking up into the face of an angel he hadn't seen in several ages.

"I can't believe you ended up with the Angel of Light for a mentor. Guess I shouldn't have passed up that old cabin," said Alexander.

"Oh, I'm sure things have worked out well for you. Where are you working these days?"

The giant angel replied, "I'm working under the Archangel Michael; strategic planning. Lots of theoretical stuff. How about you?"

"Department of Celestial Fellowship, under Barnabas."

"Really, I would think with a mentor like Lucifer, you would have...umm, well, that sounds very important."

Malachi wasn't convinced Alexander really believed that based on his tone. "It certainly keeps me busy," Malachi said. "Anyway, Elohim is pleased with our efforts, and we're blessed to have an opportunity to serve Him."

Alexander said, "I guess you're off to serve Him now then. I am going to the Special Announcement at the Assembly Chamber. Too bad we can't visit more."

Malachi pulled the invitation from his satchel. He couldn't help himself. The shocked expression on Alexander's face was priceless. Malachi grinned. "I guess we will get that chance after all."

"Guess you're right. We might as well stick together then. Come on, let's go."

With that, the pair took to the sky, joining the glowing flood of heavenly host heading for the fourth heaven.

* * * * * *

Malachi and Alexander found themselves walking up Servant's Heart Avenue when they arrived in the Fourth Heaven. This main thoroughfare transected the city sector of the fourth heaven, cutting a path from the southern end of the city to the Mount of the Assembly in the recesses of the north. Along the way, they would run directly past the Archangel Michael's office.

Alexander asked, "Since we are passing my office, would you mind if we make one stop? I need to check in on one special assignment the Archangel has asked me to do."

"Sure, and I'd like to see where you work."

Malachi had walked this street on many occasions in the past. For some reason, something looked different to him. However, no matter how hard he tried, he couldn't quite put his finger on it. Finally, as they walked past the Department of Celestial Communications, it jumped out at him. He stopped and turned to look back in the direction from which they had come. He whispered, "I see it now. They are in front of every Department Headquarters."

"What did you say?" asked Alexander.

"Oh, I was just noticing something. Did you see those angels standing at the entrance of each of the Department Headquarters?"

"Sure, I'm the one who ordered them to stand there. Well, actually, Michael did that, but I'm the one who carried out the order for him."

"What is that strange satchel they have around their waist? I've never seen one before."

Alexander laughed. "That's no satchel. It's called a scabbard and it holds a sword."

"A sword?" Malachi repeated, having never heard of such a thing.

"Better I show you." Alexander took him over to one of the guards standing in a front doorway and asked to see his sword. The guard drew a long silver blade from the scabbard and handed it over. "These were made by the finest blacksmiths in heaven." Alexander gripped the golden hilt with two hands and swung the sharp end through the air. "It's an instrument the guards can use to prevent angels from entering those buildings if they aren't supposed to do so."

"We've never needed anyone to do that before. Why now?"

Alexander whispered, "I don't know. We really aren't supposed to ask. I just know I'm supposed to make sure the assigned angels are watching their building at the appropriate time. That's actually why I said we had to go to the Archangel Michael's office on the way to the Assembly Chamber. I was assigned the task of making sure the guards at each building south of the Archangel's offices were doing their job along the way. Tell you what, when we get to the office, I'll show you something else we are doing that is out of the ordinary."

When they arrived at the Archangel Michael's office, Alexander led Malachi around the building to a small park in the rear. As they approached, Malachi heard an unfamiliar sound. It sounded like…the silver buckles used to fasten the flags to the draw ropes when they banged up against the flagpole…only much louder. When he finally got to a spot where he could see what was happening, he couldn't believe his eyes. Angels, like those who were standing out in front of each department headquarters, had drawn their swords and were swinging at each other. As the sword of one angel struck that of another, they produced a deafening, high pitched sound. Occasionally, one of the angels would be struck by the blade and let out a strange cry.

"It looks like they are trying to hit each other. Why?" asked Malachi.

"I've been told they're just practicing, but still, sometimes an angel gets struck by a sword, and they then cry out like that. I haven't been hit yet, so I don't know what it feels like."

"I would say based on what that last angel did, it doesn't feel good."

Alexander grabbed Malachi's arm and said, "Look over there. It's the other tool we've been told to use to stop angels from going where we don't want them to go. Well, it's really two tools used together…a bow and an arrow. The bow throws the arrow at whatever you want to stop."

For several minutes, Malachi and Alexander watched the angels practicing. Some pulled back their bows and shot arrows into targets. Others clashed their swords together. Finally, Alexander nudged Malachi and informed him that they needed to get going to the Assembly Chamber. As they walked away, Malachi struggled to process all he'd just witnessed. So deep in thought was Malachi as they made their way to the Mount of the Assembly that he continued straight when Alexander turned.

"Hey Malachi, this is our turn. Where's your head at today?"

Rejoining Alexander, Malachi said, "It doesn't make sense. Why would the Archangel Michael order such training, and why would Elohim want to stop angels from entering those buildings?"

Alexander only shrugged. "The King has never tried to stop us from going anywhere before."

Malachi said, "I'll ask Barnabas when I get back to our offices. Maybe he knows."

The young angels navigated the golden streets of the great city, continuing to make their way toward the Mount of the Assembly. Glistening in the light of the King's glory, only the Holy Mount rivaled the Assembly for ornate beauty. Twelve spires rose into the air, capped by eternal flames leaping even higher still. Though not needed to light the surrounding opal façade of the structure amid the ever-present glory of Elohim, the eternal flames offered up a pleasing aroma of praise to Yahweh. It was He, God the Father, who sat on His throne in the highest heaven on the Holy Mount. There He received praise from the ever-present Seraphim and from select members of the Department of Worship, even as the adoration of every other angel rose with the sweet fragrance from the spires of the Assembly.

Within the Great Hall of the Assembly Chamber, elevated high above the gallery, stood the throne from which Yeshua, God the Son, reigned over His eternal kingdom. Though Malachi had seen the towering walls of the Assembly numerous times and even stood beneath its flying buttresses on several ceremonial occasions, never before had he been asked to enter.

Humbly, he whispered to himself, "Not sure why they asked me to take part in this announcement. Whatever the reason, I hope I represent the department well. All can say is, 'I am blessed beyond measure.'"

In reality, every angel in heaven was blessed beyond measure. All received a precious gift, life, when they were created. Not just life. Life in the presence of his Creator. In return for this treasure, the angels of heaven served and worshipped the King unreservedly.

The closer Malachi got to the Assembly Chamber, the more awestruck he became. Streets of gold. Gates of pearl. Pillars of finely polished marble. Precious gems and luminescent stones lined windows through which a radiant light glowed without the slightest flicker.

Malachi patted Alexander on the shoulder and said, "Oh, the glory of Yeshua. Never ceasing, unwavering."

"Yes, it's awe inspiring."

"May my gratitude for all He's done for me be as resolute as the light of His glory." He couldn't wait to see His King face-to-face.

CHAPTER SEVEN

THE ANNOUNCEMENT

"Pride goes before destruction, and a haughty spirit before a fall."
Proverbs 16:18

The Assembly Chamber

L ucifer entered through one of the twelve sets of large exterior doors. Each door was made from black pearl inlaid with precious stones and gems. He stepped with excitement across the floor of the broad entry hall, with its polished gold tiles inset with diamonds the size of a clinched fist. In the corner of the chamber, members of the worship team softly chanted, "Holy, Holy, Holy is the Lord God Almighty, Who was, Who is, and Who is to come."

Lucifer tried to imagine what the angels might chant about him on the day he was seated next to Elohim as a joint ruler of the kingdom.

Without warning, the Archangel Michael interrupted Lucifer's daydream. "Do you know what the King plans to announce today? It has to be big for Him to pull us away from our duties."

Next to him, the Archangel Gabriel added, "I hope it is, and I hope the King gives me permission to share it with the rest of the heavenly host."

Lucifer thought, *Oh yes, it's important, and long overdue. For many millennia, you have both acted as if we are equals. Time for you two to finally recognize me as your superior in every way.*

They entered the throne room and were immediately bathed in the glory of Elohim, their individual radiance being drowned out in the splendor of His majesty. Each angel acted as a mirror to reflect the magnificently pure, white light of His holiness around the chamber. Every angel fixed their eyes on the source of the brilliance, Elohim, and marveled at His splendor.

Every angel, but one.

Lucifer looked at himself and whispered under his breath, "Look at my splendor. In this chamber, I shine with the glory of Elohim. No one can distinguish between the King and me."

His heart, swollen with pride, made its final pivot. "I will ascend above the heights of the clouds, the presence of the Holy Spirit in the higher heavens. Once higher than Ruach Elohim, I will reside on the Holy Mount rather than simply working there among the fiery stones."

An idea, first meditated upon in his mind, had made its way to his heart. Now, it coalesced into a core belief, a presupposition. "I will make myself like the Most High, a god overseeing every level of heaven. After all, it's who I AM."

* * * * * *

Just as the doors were being closed by the King's Honor Guard, Malachi and Alexander slipped into the Assembly Chamber. While Alexander grabbed a seat in the back of the chamber, Malachi was forced to find the next available seat. Despite his attempts to keep from drawing attention to himself, his tardiness meant the only open chair happened to be very close to the three angels at the center of attention for this meeting. With chin tucked and stooping as low to the ground as possible, Malachi sat behind Michael, Gabriel, and Lucifer.

He thought, *Best seats in the house, unless you're trying to remain inconspicuous.* Malachi felt his face flush as several angels turned in his direction, looks of disapproval crossing their faces.

* * * * * *

Just as Michael, Gabriel, and Lucifer finished settling into their normal positions in front of the throne terrace in the Assembly, the King's herald stepped forward to call the meeting to order. In a loud voice, he proclaimed, "Praise the Lord! Praise the Lord from the heavens; praise Him in the heights! Praise Him, all His angels; praise Him, all His hosts!"

In a loud voice, all of the angels present in the throne room answered, "Praise the Lord! Glory to God in the highest!"

At this, Yeshua rose from His throne, stepped to the front of the elevated terrace and began to address the angels who bowed before Him.

"Michael, Gabriel, and Lucifer...We brought you here to announce Our next great step in creation. You three are among My most highly respected angels, each of you having consistently distinguished yourself in your service to Me. Because of that loyalty and devotion, We've decided you each will be given a new role related directly to Our next step in the process of creation.

"Before I describe those roles to you, let Me describe the plan. Before We purposed in Our hearts to create any of you angels, We foreknew and predetermined all that has transpired from that moment until now and out into eternity in the future. This also includes a special period during eternity which is marked by a beginning and an end; a period which involves a new concept We will call 'time.' This 'time' will be much more important during the next step of creation.

"This eternal plan, including the portion defined by time, is designed to glorify Us while giving one among Our creation the greatest treasure of all...an intimate, love-based relationship with Us. There has always been a separation between Us; We as Creator and you as Our creation. It is Our intention to bridge that gap by raising up one from among creation to both represent and rule over the rest of creation. You have been the most highly decorated of My created beings, so it would seem fitting that such a representative and ruler would come from among the three of you."

Lucifer looked to his left and right at the excited faces of Michael and Gabriel. *Don't get your hopes up too high, you two. Elohim previously made me Overseer of the Garden of Eden. Thereafter, He rightfully saw fit to promote me to service on the Holy Mount. He has rewarded me at every turn and in every conceivable manner. He would be foolish to grant this new assignment to one of you. What have you accomplished apart from Him? Besides, He says His plan follows a pre-determined course. Once He makes me the head of the heavenly host, dominion over a new creation seems the next logical step.*

Lucifer's pride welled up within him. *Once I am above all of creation, I will continue to rise. I will be like the Most High. It's just a matter of time before I am recognized as a god.*

Lucifer looked up. With his mind back in the Assembly Chamber and out of his daydream of self-worship, he became cognizant of Yeshua's gaze. Lucifer thought to himself, *Caught You looking at me. Now I know it is true. You can never keep Your eyes off someone You are about to honor.*

As if on cue, Yeshua moved directly on to their new roles. "I will start with you,

Michael. As My Archangel in charge of My Honor Guard, you will now have a new charge to protect. Gabriel, you will have a message to declare. Lucifer..." The King paused. Lucifer was ready to explode with excitement. *This is the moment for which I've been waiting since my creation day. In fact, it is the moment I've deserved for ages. The recognition and position to which a being of my grandeur and beauty should naturally attain. I did it by myself. I willed it, and it happened. All because I AM.*

Yeshua repeated, "Lucifer..." There was something odd in the way He said his name; something almost emotional. *The King is overwhelmed. He can't get the words out.*

Finally, Yeshua continued, "Lucifer, it is to you that I grant the greatest role in this next step in Our plans for creation."

This is it. This is the culmination of all that it is to be created. This is where I take the next step in my progression to godhood.

Elohim's voice resonated throughout the chamber even as His glory filled every shadowy nook. "We have decided to make a new being, one more special than any We have previously created. Their uniqueness comes in that they shall be made in Our own image, according to Our likeness. This We have never done before, not even with you, My faithful servants. Furthermore, We decided to create these beings in two different forms, one called 'male' and the other called 'female.' This is significant, for in this We shall give them the ability to reproduce themselves according to their own kind. Mankind will exist for a little while lower than you, My angelic host. But eventually, We will raise them up to be even greater. They will exist not just as creatures, but they shall be Our friends."

"In fact," Yahweh interjected, "eventually I will make them joint heirs with Yeshua as My adopted children." Each word seared the heart of Lucifer and filled him with indignation.

Murmuring passed through the audience, as Elohim's announcement took the angels completely by surprise.

Elohim watched the reaction of His angels. *We will create mankind to be a frail creature. We do this for a reason. All will know that the greatness he achieves comes neither by his own power nor his own wisdom. Instead, all will know that man achieves greatness by My Spirit alone, as do you all."

Wonder and awe filled the air as Michael and Gabriel rejoiced at Elohim's plan and at this new creation. Worship poured from their lips as they raised their voices declaring, "Glory to God in the highest, and peace among mankind with whom

He is well pleased."

All lifted praises to Yahweh, Yeshua, and Ruach Elohim for Their great wisdom. Every angel but one.

Yeshua said, "Lucifer, as my Guardian Cherub and former Overseer of My Garden of Eden, your service to Me has always been exemplary. I now give you the great privilege of…serving these new beings. You will both protect and help guide them as they grow in wisdom and in knowledge. Help them learn how to properly worship Me. It is a great task I entrust to your hands, for they will be My beloved creation, experiencing what only they will ever know: My love."

Lucifer could barely believe what he was hearing. *Has the King gone completely mad? How dare He reduce me to the manservant of a helpless fawn? I should be greater than the angels; I should be joint heir with Yeshua on the Mount of the Assembly. I should be like the Most High God.* Lucifer looked up at Yeshua just in time to catch the King's eyes gazing down on him again. Lucifer quickly joined his angelic brothers in voicing words of praise to Elohim, the Godhead Trinity. While his mouth spoke the words, his heart seethed within him. This too did not go unnoticed.

Elohim thought as He watched Lucifer's reaction, *What you allow into your head gets into your heart, and what enters your heart eventually comes out of your mouth and through your hands. When an individual stops storing up My words in his heart, that individual becomes susceptible to sinning against Me both in thought and in deed.*

CHAPTER EIGHT

ADRAMELECH

"Let no one deceive you with empty words, for because of these things the wrath of God comes upon the sons of disobedience."

Ephesians 5:6

M alachi arrived at the Department of Celestial Fellowship early, eager to share with Barnabas what had transpired at the Assembly Chamber during the big announcement. As he rounded the corner and entered his workstation, he was surprised to find Barnabas already present and sitting in his chair, a very serious look on his face. "What in the world did you do when you met with Lucifer?"

Malachi braced himself for unexpected bad news. "I don't know. Well, I did walk around his office, but I was only admiring the artwork."

"You did what?" Barnabas watched as his star associate squirmed about, trying to figure out what he'd done wrong.

Finally, Barnabas could stand it no more, his disappointed look giving way to laughter. As he did the day before, Barnabas reached into his satchel and produced yet another envelope.

Malachi quickly scanned the front and realized it bore the seal of the Department of Worship.

"What is this?"

The scraggly old angel simply said, "Seems your little visit with Lucifer didn't go as badly as you thought."

Shocked, Malachi tore into the envelope. He read aloud, "From Adramelech, Director of Operations to the Angel of Light. Malachi...instructed by Lucifer to meet with you regarding open associate role within our department. Come highly recommended by current supervisor at Department of Celestial Fellowship. Needing to fill role immediately. Can you meet me at..."

"I've already told Adramelech you can make it," Barnabas said before Malachi could finish reading the invitation.

"Did you have something to do with this?" asked Malachi.

"Well, that really doesn't matter. What does is that you seem to have been granted your wish. So, go. Make the most of your opportunity."

Malachi tried to contain his elation.

"Oh, go ahead and let it out. I did when I saw the envelope arrive," Barnabas said with a smile. "I'm excited for you. I've never heard of so much good news coming to one angel within such a short period of time."

After a few moments of unbridled celebration during which the two angels danced in circles both on the ground and in the air, Barnabas finally said, "OK, give me a few hours of your best work so we don't fall completely behind. You can fill me in on Elohim's announcement at the Assembly later. I'm sure I'll receive an official statement soon anyway."

Following an hour of unproductive effort on Malachi's part, Barnabas could endure his subordinate's distracted gaze no more. He jokingly commanded, "That's it, Malachi. Get out of here; you're no good to me at this point." Laughing, he added, "You did better than I would have done under the circumstances."

"Are you sure?"

"Don't make me start second-guessing myself. The work can wait. Get going."

"Yes, Sir." As Malachi walked away, he turned back to Barnabas and said, "Blessed Beyond Measure."

Barnabas clapped his hands. "Blessed Beyond Measure. Indeed, we are all blessed beyond measure."

Pausing at his locker to gather his things, Malachi reached into his pouch and pulled out the invitation bearing the seal of the Department of Worship. Slowly and carefully, for at the least the hundredth time, he read the invitation from Adramelech.

I can't believe I have an interview for an associate position at the Department of Worship. I haven't been at the Department of Celestial Fellowship very long. He whispered, "Elohim, thank you for this opportunity. Please give me wisdom as I speak with Adramelech. May You be honored by all I say and do, and may Your will be done above all else." He closed his locker and made for the streets. He would spirit leap close to the Art District and walk from there. That way he would have time to regain his energy before the interview began.

* * * * * *

Turning the corner just east of the Art District, Malachi moved as quickly as he could to the second building on the left, a satellite office for the Department of Worship. Once inside, he took his seat among myriad other angels hoping to begin a new chapter in their own existence. He watched as angel after angel entered and left the main office. Though the wait was short, eternity seemed to pass before Malachi heard his name called.

"Malachi. Department of Celestial Fellowship."

"Here. Coming."

Thrusting his hand into the air while simultaneously leaping from his chair sent Malachi into full flight.

"I can see someone's excited to meet the Director." A smirk flashed across the assistant's face as Malachi carefully returned to the ground.

"Uh, yes, Sir. Well…" Malachi knelt to gather his things now strewn across the floor. He couldn't think of anything else to say. He only hoped his waiting room exploits would remain in their place of origin.

No such luck. As soon as they entered Adramelech's office, the assistant seemed already intent on culling out an unworthy candidate. He announced with a chuckle, "This is Malachi from the Department of Celestial Fellowship. I know you're running late, Director, so—"

Scrolls on the desk in front of Malachi found a new home on the floor, carried there by the wind produced when Adramelech's large chair spun around to face its next guest. When it settled into place, Malachi found himself looking into the eyes of Adramelech, Lucifer's Director of Operations. The young angel's thoughts wandered as he processed the appearance of his host, the one who seemingly now controlled the next step in his development.

Though he appeared about as tall as Malachi, nothing else about Adramelech's features would command a room, at least not in the traditional sense. Long tufts of disheveled hair fell from his head and down his back. Rather than looking like the glorious flowing mane of the *o-io*, which ran across the grasslands of the second heaven in family groups called prides, his hair looked like that of the *khah-MOHR*, which though similar in shape to the powerful steeds of the range, were never mistaken for one another in appearance or grace due to their bucktoothed mouths, awkward gait, and boisterous vocalizations. Adding to his odd appearance was his large nose with flaring nostrils. In what appeared to be an attempt to draw attention away from his less attractive features, Adramelech wore an outfit which actually bore the long, wispy plumes of the beautiful *tah-VAHS* birds, with their unmistakable iridescent blue and green coloring and distinctive black dot. The effect was the opposite of that which was intended as the outfit only made his odd appearance more pronounced.

Meanwhile, Malachi snapped back into reality moments later when he noticed the director's assistant making his way towards his superior. The potential saboteur of Malachi's career leaned toward Adramelech and whispered something in his ear. Adramelech seemed to suppress a laugh.

Great, my first significant interview in ages, and I blow it in the lobby. Despite his rough beginning, to Malachi's surprise, he wasn't immediately ushered to the exit. Instead, Adramelech asked him to step into his office and take a seat.

"So, you're Malachi. I've been waiting to speak with you."

Malachi hesitated. This was not at all what he'd expected. No response came to mind.

"Well, for someone working in the Department of Celestial Fellowship, you sure don't come across as very gregarious."

Again, the young angel struggled to begin his part of the conversation. Just as the Director was about to share another pithy comment, Malachi's mouth overcame its paralysis. "Sorry, Sir. It's just that I'm only now recovering from my unplanned flight around your lobby. I'd like not to repeat the feat with my mouth now that I'm actually here speaking with you. After all, communication is supposed to be my forte. I'd like to show I can at least control that, even if I struggle to control my enthusiasm."

Adramelech let out a chuckle. "Well, I guess being enthusiastic likely helps in your line of work. Barnabas told me you were one of his best. So, dazzle me. Why should we recommend to the King that you be made an associate in the Department of Worship?"

The next few minutes were a blur. No sooner had Malachi run through his resume than did the questions from the Director seem to pivot. No longer were they focused on how his activities at the Department of Celestial Fellowship might align with the duties of an associate at the Department of Worship. Instead, they delved into the vast network he had developed over the ages during which he'd served in his current post.

"So, you're saying you have a personal relationship with the leaders of the first and fourth provincial assemblies?" asked Adramelech.

"Yes, Sir. In fact, I actually just organized and implemented a gathering between their two branches."

"Hmmm. Burijas and Dahaka. Strong angels. They would mean much to our..."

Adramelech stopped short of completing his statement. "So, Malachi. After we finish up here, do you have a few moments you can spare for a second interview with the Primicerius, himself?"

Without hesitation, Malachi answered in the affirmative.

Adramelech continued, "I have to tell you, I don't believe we will have any interest in you as an associate in the department. Your level of experience is simply not enough for this associate position."

Malachi was caught completely off guard. At first, he started to backtrack over his statements in a vain attempt to resurrect a fading opportunity. Then, it occurred to him that he'd been asked to take an interview with Lucifer. He asked, "Didn't you say I have a second interview? How can I have a second interview when you have already ruled me out for the position?"

"I said you aren't qualified for an associate position. Did I mention I want you to take part in the interviews for the Chief of Staff to the Angel of Light? You would prefer that role, would you not?"

"Absolutely, Sir." Again, Malachi was in shock. Adramelech wrapped up the interview and ushered Malachi back into the lobby. As Adramelech started to close the door, he called out,

"Oh, Malachi. Please do control your enthusiasm a bit when we call your name next time."

"I'll do my best, Sir."

CHAPTER NINE

TWISTED AND CONFUSED

"For the company of the godless is barren, and fire
consumes the tents of the corrupt. They conceive mischief and
bring forth iniquity, and their mind prepares deception."

Job 15:34-35

Malachi wrestled throughout the day with why Lucifer and Adramelech would consider him a good candidate for the Chief of Staff position. An associate position he could understand. Perhaps he could impress someone in the department with his creative ideas and work ethic, then eventually get a chance at a promotion within the department. But the Chief of Staff? Really?

He whispered to himself, "But these are the wisest angels in Elohim's kingdom. Surely, they must see something in me they feel is suited for this role. I have to trust in their wisdom." Lowering his head, he prayed for Ruach Elohim to still his spirit and to simply allow him to do his best.

When he finished, he opened the door.

Malachi entered the office expecting a long wait behind many well-qualified candidates. Instead, he was struck by just how few were present in the lobby.

A muscular angel who dwarfed Malachi quickly crossed the room. His towering presence rose skyward to a head full of jet black, shoulder-length hair cascading down in waves.

Despite his brilliant appearance, the angel had a weathered look. It was as though he had spent years in a desert environment enduring the blasting heat of a nearby star and unrelenting winds. Still, he carried himself with an authoritative air. *Certainly, this angel possesses the characteristics Lucifer would be looking for in a Chief of Staff.* Malachi's heart sank as he contemplated his chances of outcompeting this angel for the role.

The conversation between the two began pleasantly enough with a simple introduction. "I am Moloch. Who are you?"

Malachi responded in kind and then immediately went back to reviewing his credentials in hopes that this giant would lose interest in further conversation. He was not so lucky.

"Do you really think your resume holds the secret to obtaining this position?" said Moloch, a sneer crossing his face. "Perhaps in a universe where any of us really has a choice in what we do. But in this existence, the only thing that really matters is loyalty. Without it, none of us stands a chance of getting ahead and establishing a name for ourselves."

Malachi was astounded at Moloch's brash comments. But instead of turning away, Malachi said, "I have no interest in establishing a name for myself. Glorifying the King and elevating His name is my only goal. And how can you say you have no opportunity for advancement? Look at where we both are. We're in the office of the Director of Operations to the Angel of Light, with a chance to become Lucifer's Chief of Staff."

"Oh yes," responded Moloch, "We both have a chance at this position. But, who do we have to thank for the opportunity?"

Malachi anwered, "Everyone knows every good gift comes from our Lord and King, Elohim."

Moloch chuckled. "Look at your invitation to this interview. Does it mention the office of the King, God, Yahweh, Elohim, anywhere on it? No. Do you think God is really concerned about a lowly angel like you? Your credentials don't even warrant a second glance at a possible promotion for ages. And look at me." Moloch touched a hand to his puffed-out chest. "I've long-served the King loyally, only wishing for the chance to achieve an Archangel status at some point. All I ever hear is 'well-done, good and faithful servant.' And yet, after all I've done, only Lucifer seems to really notice my dedication."

Malachi took a long look at the invitation Adramelech had given him. Upon examination, the card did indeed hold no mention of the King. In fact, though the interview was being held at Adramelech's office, the invitation stated that it was from Lucifer personally. Malachi assumed the invitation had been ordered by the King, but now he clearly recognized that hadn't been the case.

Confusion scaled the ramparts of his mind. *Does Elohim see me as only a lowly staff member while Lucifer sees me as potentially more? Is it possible he has something to offer me that Elohim won't?*

He quickly stopped himself and focused on what he knew to be true. *Wait. God's ways are always just and fair. I might not always like His timing, but when He moves, it always proves to be at the ideal moment.*

Though Malachi could still hear the Spirit of God guiding him into truth, Moloch's words seemed to muffle the Spirit's voice. As Malachi strained to hear the Spirit's words of wisdom, the thunderous comments of Moloch drove the roots of confusion deep into his being. The crafty angel chided, "God isn't interested in seeing members of His heavenly host, such as us, achieve our full potential. Look at your resume. How many millennia has it been since your creation day?

"Hard to recall, isn't it? Well, He really doesn't care. To Him, we are merely servants to do His bidding. He promises blessings for those who worship Him the way He feels He deserves, but what does He give us in return? Oh, only the opportunity to worship Him more, to serve Him more, and to wait for His Grace to finally see fit to reward our loyalty to Him." The sarcasm in Moloch's voice was undeniable.

Just then, Adramelech's assistant called for Moloch to enter the Director's office for his interview. Moloch entered to the extended hand of Adramelech. As the door closed, the Director pulled Moloch close and gave the loyal servant of his king a congratulatory embrace.

Malachi sat in his chair, bewildered by what had just taken place. *I thought Elohim wanted me to achieve my potential. Has He just been holding me back?*

Though Moloch's poisonous ideas were hard for the naïve angel to digest, they had disrupted Malachi's defenses. His mind wandered to thoughts of new positions and achievements, whether or not he was being held back by Elohim, and if Lucifer was more likely to promote him than was the King. Self gained a foothold, and Ruach Elohim's voice became muffled. Fertile ground for the manipulative words of those working to sway Malachi from the King's ranks.

* * * * * *

Through a crack in the door leading to the back offices of the department, a mysterious figure watched and listened for just the right moment to escalate his attack on Malachi. As he did, he heard Malachi whisper to himself, "Is it possible Lucifer sees more in me than does Elohim? I really want this position, but if I'm competing with angels like Moloch, do I really stand a chance at all?"

* * * * * *

In the silence after Moloch's departure, an angel seated on the other side of the lobby rose to his feet and glided forward into the vacated space. Unlike the former angel, this celestial being was altogether beautiful. Ivory white wings extended behind a face and body which looked chiseled from the finest granite by the Master Artisan Himself. His external beauty was rivaled only by a larger-than-life charisma. "Well, Sir. Looks like you are quite popular. Thought I should meet you for myself."

As the angel extended his hand to introduce himself, Malachi felt an odd sensation. His hands dampened and his heartbeat quickened. Never before had he felt such insecurity. But then again, *He wants to meet me. Does he see the same something in me that Adramelech saw this morning?* Malachi's discerning spirit relented as his natural humility gave way to an elevated sense of self.

The beautiful angel smiled and said, "I'm Semiazas, current Director of Communications for the King's third Provincial Assembly. With whom do I have the pleasure of speaking?"

Malachi felt himself blush as he made his introductions to this ornate angel.

More flattering words poured like fine wine from the lips of Semiazas. "I knew as soon as you entered the room you must be the front-runner for this position. I don't even have to see your resume to tell you are just what Lucifer wants for his Chief of Staff. Strong sense of self-worth, an independent thinker, and able to quickly decipher the true nature of circumstances here in the heavenly places. Obviously, I don't stand a chance against you in this interview. Please remember me if you find yourself in need of staff members."

"May I ask, why do feel that way about me? We just met. That other angel, Moloch, seemed to think I didn't stand a chance against him. "

"Don't you see? They sought you out instead of the other way around. Sure, the rest of us have great resumes, but we had to apply for this position. You didn't. They want you for sure. Moloch was trying to get you to doubt yourself. After all, Lucifer wants someone who can think for himself without the barriers established for us since our creation. New ideas. Fresh thinking. Someone who will show the same kind of loyalty to Lucifer that he has shown in offering this great opportunity."

Malachi thought, *Semiazas might be right. I was sought after by Lucifer. Moloch must feel threatened by me. I have been a star in the Department of Celestial Fellowship for a long time. Lucifer saw that, and these other angels see it too.*

Once he started to accept the concept of his own value, Malachi couldn't suppress the question that had been building inside him. *If God knows all things, why couldn't He see my true abilities?*

"Bet you're wondering why the King can't see what we all see. Think about it. God is omniscient So if He knows how good you are, why wouldn't He give you the same chance Lucifer is about to extend? There's only one explanation: God knows you deserve this position. He just doesn't want you to have it."

It all seemed undeniable. *God's been holding me back. Lucifer can see that, and he wants me to be all I can be. If Lucifer gives me the chance, I'll give him all I have. I'll give him all I am.*

"Now you're thinking." Semiazas seemed able to read his thoughts even though Malachi knew only God could do such a thing. Still, it was uncanny. *It must be the wisdom of these angels. They must be wiser than Elohim thinks they are. Makes sense...seems I am as well. Although it's strange He doesn't put a stop to their efforts. I'll have to watch my own thoughts to keep God from knowing what I now understand. It must be truth to trust in Self.*

Honey dripping from the comb can be so tempting. Such were the words and twisted logic of Semiazas. Malachi now found them easier to swallow. With his defenses down, the idea of Self, which had seemed so ludicrous in that run-down cabin on the backside of Eden, now suddenly seemed to have merit.

Semiazas grinned as Malachi whispered, "I am more than Elohim allows me to be. He created me to be the 'One.' These angels have shown me I am the 'One.' I am the 'One' Lucifer wants as his Chief of Staff...maybe even more.

As with Moloch, Malachi's conversation with Semiazas ended almost as quickly as it started. The angel was called to enter Adramelech's office for his interview. Malachi wished him luck as he left. Semiazas had been so warm and cordial. And yet, he knew in his heart that he really didn't mean it. Doubts gave way to optimism as Malachi now knew in his heart that an offer for this lofty position had to be only moments away.

Malachi now wanted Lucifer's Chief of Staff position more than anything. Previously, he had looked forward to worshipping and serving the King. Now for the first time, there was another ambition filling Malachi's heart. He would get ahead by serving Lucifer. As he waited his turn to enter Adramelech's office, he said to himself, "I can serve the King loyally while also being loyal to Lucifer. He is the Angel of Light, and he serves the King as well. He just wants to get ahead at the same time. There's nothing wrong with that. I can do the same."

* * * * * *

The seeds of Self, first planted in Malachi's head by Lucifer during his mentorship, then watered by Moloch and Semiazas, now found fertile soil for the first time in Malachi's heart.

Roots were beginning to spread, and he was perilously close to giving himself over to Self completely.

The orchestrator of Malachi's abrupt fall rubbed his hands together as a grin washed over Adramelech's face. All that was left was to seal the deal and to add Malachi to the throng of angels now following Self…who called Lucifer their king.

CHAPTER TEN

WHOSE WORD IS TRUTH

"Sanctify them by the truth; Your word is truth."
John 17: 17

As the moments lingered, Malachi felt an odd sensation. Normally, the passage of time was meaningless to him. It was simply imperceptible to those with an eternal mindset. But now, as Malachi pondered the words of Moloch and Semiazas and considered the possibilities of advancing in his career, he became increasingly anxious to begin his interview. Half in preparation and half in distraction, Malachi decided to take a few moments to review how he would respond to some of the anticipated questions he would receive once taken back. His intense focus betrayed him to the solitary figure who slipped into the chair next to his own.

The obscure features and stealth-like manner of Malachi's uninvited companion shocked the young angel when the form finally captured his attention. Never before had he encountered one of the heavenly host with such an appearance. The angel's eyes were dark and empty, like solid black orbs. Caught in their gaze, Malachi felt paralyzed.

He held his breath, unable to shake the strange feelings coursing through his body. A shiver ran up his spine, his heart began to race, and Malachi felt an unusual desire to run from the room. He wondered what he would do if the angel asked him a question. *I can't begin to think of what might proceed from . . .* Malachi hesitated in mid-thought, then finished . . . *its lips.* He couldn't believe he had such a thought concerning an angel created by Elohim, and yet, what sat next to him seemed so grotesque that he couldn't bring himself to consider it as one of the heavenly host.

When the door to Adramelech's office opened and his name was called, Malachi heard himself audibly exhale. Anxiety over an interview seemed like nothing compared to the oppressive feeling of emptiness and foul stench emitted from the specter.

Malachi quickly stumbled toward the office of the Director and into a large chamber. He had no idea that his eternal fate rested in the next few hours. After countless years of loyal service to his Creator, what would take place in the next few moments could establish what Malachi's existence would be like for the rest of eternity.

Lost in his thoughts and waiting for Adramelech to finish escorting Semiazas out the back door, Malachi was abruptly stirred back into the moment by the muffled words of the angel guarding the entryway. So surprised was Malachi to be addressed by this angel that he completely missed what the guard tried to say to him.

"Sir, can you hear me?" the guard asked again. "Whose word is truth? Can you still tell the difference? Whose word is truth?"

"What did you say?" asked Malachi. Countless moments of revealed truth, reinforced during the ages of his loyal service to Elohim, broke through the murkiness of his most recent thoughts. The King's words echoed over and over in his ears. My word is truth...*My word is truth...My word is truth.*

Malachi thought, *I know Your word is truth, but You don't seem to care or even know about my situation. You are so distant when I need You right here, right now. Lucifer seems to see more in me than You do. Why is that? Could Lucifer's words be just as true?*

Before Malachi could uncover why the guard had asked such a question, Adramelech arrived to usher Malachi into the main office for his interview. As they shook hands and moved towards the nearby table and chairs, a side door to the office swung open. In stepped the Angel of Light, his intense eyes locked on Malachi's. The young angel shivered and felt uneasy in his old mentor's presence.

Lucifer and Adramelech each placed a hand on one of Malachi's shoulders. Half escorting, half shoving, they pushed him into a chair in the back corner of the office.

Adramelech said, "We are certainly glad to see you. As you know, you are here to interview for the Chief of Staff position. Certainly, it is quite a leap from your previous role at the Department of Celestial Fellowship. In fact, it's quite a step up from the associate role here in the Department of Worship for which you interviewed earlier. Regardless, I saw something unique in that meeting which suggested I should take a chance on you."

"I thank you for that, Sir. I'll do my best to make you glad you did."

"Of course, you are competing for this position with some very experienced and well-respected angels. Let's just talk for a while and see what happens. No promises, but know it is a huge honor to progress to this point."

Is he saying they're happy I'm here because I'm special in some way, or are they trying to cushion the blow when they tell me I'm out of the running?

Malachi decided he was in for a fight if he was going be offered the position. He thought through his past work experiences, his efforts to promote unity among the angels, his many long hours of service to the King and to the community of angels. While all of it was honorable work and bettered the fellowship between angels in the heavenly places, it seemed so trivial compared to what Moloch and Semiazas must have presented. Malachi wracked his brain searching for any hidden detail that would make what he did seem worthy to become Chief of Staff to the Angel of Light.

From the confusion of his own thoughts, Malachi suddenly heard Lucifer's voice. So irresistible was its tone and cadence, he found himself lost within its melodious frame. He missed the actual words of Lucifer's question. Embarrassed, Malachi asked, "Sir, would you mind repeating that?"

Lucifer never blinked, but simply stated, "I hear you are some sort of star within the Department of Celestial Fellowship. How did your colleagues come to feel that way?"

Malachi couldn't believe the question had been so simple. "Well, I guess it must relate to my having received numerous awards usually reserved for individuals with significantly greater tenure in an assignment." Malachi was jubilant for the opportunity to point to his service record and awards so quickly. *Good start.*

"Hmmm..." said Adramelech, nodding his head. "So, what awards did you receive, and why do you think you won them over your more experienced colleagues?"

"Well, Sir, I've actually received three different awards. First, I was awarded Newcomer of the Year during my initial year in the department. There were many angels up for the award; however, I've had more documented achievements compared to any angel since the King created the heavenly host. They also polled angels from across all departments and asked about satisfaction with our efforts on their behalf. My Host-Satisfaction scores were among the highest ever recorded."

Lucifer and Adramelech both glanced at each other with a gleam in their eyes. "What were the other awards, and how did you earn them?"

This is setting up nicely. I may not have a lot of experience, but this is certainly an area in which few angels can rival me. If they want someone with a large network of angels across a lot of departments, well then, I'm their new Chief of Staff. Malachi found it hard to contain his excitement.

"I've received the King's Proclamation Award 250 times. Ten times more than any other angel in our department. To earn this honor, an angel must be recognized by his peers across all angelic departments for the inspiring way in which he performs his duties on an ongoing basis. In winning the award, I was given the opportunity to work on the Holy Mount during the Annual Celebration of Initial Creation. I served alongside the winners of the same award from the other departments to proclaim the messages of the King with Gabriel and his messenger angels.

Ultimately, it was a great reward as we developed tremendous relationships across departmental leadership teams and learned the ins-and-outs of the internal communication system used in the heavenly realm. As an aside, I actually won the award given to the fastest angel in delivering messages across all departments during the course of those award periods."

Again, Lucifer and Adramelech exchanged glances, but this time Malachi saw a subtle nod from Lucifer to Adramelech.

Finally, Malachi shared about his last award. "The King's Wreath, which I won one hundred times, is given to the angel viewed as the Most Influential among his peers and co-workers in other departments."

Smiling at Adramelech, Lucifer said, "Oh yes. That is quite an honor." Malachi began to recite the inscription on the award by memory:

"Respect and Honor. Wise angels seek both, cling to both and, as a result, receive both. Well done, good and faith servant. You have both your peers' and your King's respect and honor."

To Malachi, having the King himself make such a statement was far more valuable than anything else he had ever or would ever receive.

Lucifer and Adramelech both simultaneously repeated back, "Respect and Honor."

A few more questions followed, but Malachi had the feeling they were simply a formality. When the hour struck, Lucifer and Adramelech rose to their feet. Instead of ushering Malachi to the back exit as he had done with Semiazas, Adramelech walked around the table and pulled his chair right up to Malachi's. Lucifer stood on the other side of Malachi. The young angel had no idea what was about to happen, but he did know this was not standard interview protocol.

"Malachi, do you have any idea why Elohim placed you in the Department of Celestial Fellowship?" asked Adramelech.

Malachi had never given it any thought. He assumed it was to give him a chance to use his gifts to serve his King. *Is there something more to it than that?*

Malachi answered, "Uh, Sir, I really have no idea. I know I do it well, and I know every message I have received from the King's office is full of praise for a job well done. I've always enjoyed the job and been excited about going to it every day."

As the words came from his mouth, his mind was overwhelmed by several thoughts. *Does this sound like I am too satisfied in my current role? Are Lucifer and Adramelech looking for someone with more ambition? I want to want more, and the Chief of Staff position is certainly that.*

"Still, I know I have the skills to be more than a staff member in Celestial Fellowship. I just need the chance to demonstrate that the success I've shown in my previous positions can be transferred to a job with greater responsibility. I would appreciate the chance to show you what I can do as your Chief of Staff."

******

Lucifer placed his hand on the shoulder of Adramelech to signal that he would handle the interview from here. As if he was fishing in some celestial pool, Lucifer cast his lure in front of his targeted catch. He knew what he wanted, and he was willing to give what it would take to get it. At that moment, he wanted Malachi.

Who but a superstar in the world of celestial networking would be better to gather a large body of angels in support of a new way of thinking? Malachi was naive enough to not ask questions, ambitious enough to want to get ahead, and connected enough to be able to create a large gathering in a brief period of time.

Lucifer wanted to take advantage of Malachi's skills and position for his ultimate plan. With more angels supporting Lucifer's cause, only Elohim stood between him and true satisfaction and contentment.

"Well Malachi, you're right, in a way. God placed you in that department because He knew you would do well there. He knew He would receive great glory from your work, and you would likely be satisfied to stay and serve Him. But did He ever ask you what you really want? Did He ever set up a plan to allow you to grow and gain more, to become all you want to be?"

Malachi furrowed his brow.

Lucifer said, "I'll answer that for you. The answer is the same for all of us. No. We were created for His glory and satisfaction with no consideration of our own skills, ambitions, and capabilities. We have reached the same conclusion: we could achieve more if we were allowed by the King to do so. He holds us back because He's only concerned about Himself. The reason you are in the Department of Celestial Fellowship and have not been moved to greater things is because the King wants His will alone to be done. I believe you deserve more than that."

A lie repeated enough times eventually becomes truth both to the liar and often to those who listen to him. In an existence that had never known a lie before, the effects of Lucifer's ideas spread like wildfire. Now, Malachi was encircled by a blaze, and yet unaware of just how close to the flame he was. He sat in the presence of the father of lies, and his deceptions sounded so credible, so logical, and so true. In addition to his eloquent words, the logic of his arguments was the final element of his trap. Lucifer knew the power of selfish ambition, and he understood how to use it now as a tool to build a circle of support for his ideas.

"Let me ask you a question, Malachi. It should have been asked a long time ago. What is it that you want to achieve for yourself with this life you've been given? I know you want to serve the King, but what about *you?* What do you want at this point...for yourself? I'll tell you right now, based on your service record, you deserve it."

Malachi scratched his chin as he thought about the possibilities. "I want to lead the Department of Worship. I want to follow in your footsteps. I want to be recognized as the greatest servant of the King in the heavenly places. I want..."

Lucifer said, "And, you can have it. But I'm afraid you will only get the chance if you agree to follow me...I mean, work for me."

Lucifer could see his former protégé dangling on the edge of surrender. All it would take was the most subtle of nudges, and Malachi would move from viewing God as Provider to God as Preventer. As soon as Malachi made that turn, Lucifer knew he would have his prize, the key to unwrapping his own gift to himself.

All that was needed were more followers of his ideas on Self. Numbers large enough to bring down the King and to raise up a new one. Numbers large enough to take the Holy Mount and to name him as God and as the new king. Malachi seemed the perfect tool to reach and recruit those numbers.

Lucifer gave one last nudge. "You remember our days back in the cabin when I was your mentor?"

"Yes, of course. I remember them fondly."

"Do you remember what we tried to unravel regarding who you are?"

"Certainly, we tried to figure out why Elohim called me 'the One' on the day of my initial creation."

Lucifer smiled and gave Malachi a wink. He whispered, "I never gave up trying to figure that out. Never gave up on being able to tell you who you really are and why you are so special."

"I've never seen myself that way, but after speaking with you all today, I'm starting to believe it may be true."

Adramelech quickly chimed in, "Oh, and that's part of what makes you so special. You don't see just how talented and popular you are."

"You just do it naturally, unassuming talent and humility as well," added Lucifer. "You deserve more though, and I want to give it to you. I want to not only make you my Chief of Staff, but give you permanent access to the Holy Mount; perhaps even a sector of the heavens over which you will have dominion. Of course, I will ask for your unending loyalty if I give this to you, and it will need to stay our secret."

Lucifer stopped himself, and then said, "Speaking of secrets, are you ready to know why Elohim called you 'the One' on your initial creation day?"

"Absolutely."

"I finally figured it out. You are 'the One' who will unite the heavenly host in service of the King while pursuing your own will as well. God may not want you to pursue anything other than His will, but we all know this is not just what you deserve. It is what God would want if He weren't so fixated on Himself. He doesn't know enough to get out of His own way. In the end, it will not only be better for you, but it will turn out to be better for Him as well."

Adramelech jumped in and said to Lucifer, "In truth, Sir, I think we would all be better off if you were in control of everything. After all, if the King can't judge talent any better than this, and if He's only focused on Himself, there's no telling how much more we would achieve. We just need someone who is more focused on all of us and what we can really achieve without the King's shackles. Independence from the King is really our only chance at true freedom. It seems to me you would be the best source of freedom for us all. Malachi, you see that now, don't you?"

******

Malachi's head was aswirl. It all sounded so logical. How could something so sensible be wrong?

"So, Malachi, will you accept this position?" asked Lucifer.

Malachi couldn't believe this was happening. For so long, he wanted desperately to be offered any position at the Department of Worship. Yet now, he found himself waffling.

Lucifer pressed. "What is your answer?"

"It's such a big decision. I feel like I need to speak with Barnabas about this before I can move forward in good conscience. Thank you so much. I intend to cover this decision with prayer. I just want to make sure it is in line with the will of Elohim."

Lucifer and Adramelech quickly glanced at one another. Then Lucifer said, "Fine. Just remember, don't give it too long. Every angel would love to have this opportunity, and we have other candidates we must consider if you are not planning to accept the role."

"Don't worry, I'll have an answer to you very quickly. Thank you for considering me."

"Yes, my friend," said Lucifer. "We will be in touch."

With that, the interview ended, and Malachi walked out into the streets of His Presence. As he did, he was unexpectedly overcome by the words of His King... *My word is truth. My word is truth.*

CHAPTER ELEVEN

OVER THE LINE

*"There is a way that seems right to a man, but the
end thereof is the ways of death."*

Proverbs 16:25

Malachi stood in front of Barnabas' door, staring at it as if it was an insurmountable wall. How was he going to break the news to Barnabas? The young angel considered the scraggly old angel to be more than a supervisor.

For the first time since he began trying to speak with his old mentor, Lucifer, it occurred to Malachi that Barnabas had been filling that role for quite some time. In some ways, Malachi felt he'd gotten more from his relationship with Barnabas than he'd ever gotten from the Angel of Light. That is, until Lucifer offered him this promotion. Once again, euphoria flooded Malachi and his mind raced back to what he'd been told would be his new title should he accept the position:

Chief of Staff
Offices of the Primicerius
Department of Worship

I never knew being offered such a position was even a possibility. Yet, here I am with this opportunity staring me in the face.

He chuckled, the kind of chuckle one lets off when the anxiety of the moment leaves one with nowhere else to hide. He lightly tapped on Barnabas' door, hoping perhaps to put off the discussion until the next day. He knew there were so many aspects of his day with Lucifer and Adramelech that would be called into question by Barnabas. To Malachi's surprise, no one answered. *The old angel must have gone home early for a change.* "I guess I'll just let him know tomorrow," Malachi said as he turned to leave.

"Let me know what?"

Malachi squeezed his eyes together tightly, as if the action might prevent the inevitable from occurring. He turned to face the source of the query. When he opened his eyes, Barnabas stood in front of him in the doorway leading to the department's breakroom.

"Let you know…umm…let you know," Malachi stuttered. His mind was blank. He could think of no good way to begin the conversation.

"Oh, come out with it. Surely, you have enough topics for conversation. What did the King announce? How did your interview go with Adramelech?"

An amazing sense of relief passed through Malachi. He quickly relayed the experience of being in the Assembly Chamber, of sitting behind Michael, Gabriel, and Lucifer, and of hearing the announcement concerning the creation of man.

"So, what did the King say was the purpose behind this man?"

"Well…"

"How soon will He begin creating them?"

"Umm…"

"What role, if any, will the Department of Celestial Fellowship play?"

"Hold on. Hold on. Give me a chance to answer one question before you ask the next one."

Barnabas grinned, knowing full well he'd taken things a step too far. "Oh, sorry. Please go on…"

Malachi stared at his boss. "You want to know the purpose behind Elohim's creation of man. The King said something odd: 'We'll create mankind to be a frail creature.' He said He was doing this so all would know He was the power and the wisdom behind every good thing happening throughout the kingdom. Why would the King need to demonstrate that to all of us?"

Barnabas began his ritualistic ear scratching. "I know I asked to be frail so He would receive a different kind of praise through me. Could He be seeking more of the same from others among us? I don't know. When you spoke with Adramelech afterwards, what did he seem to think?"

For a moment, there was complete silence between them.

"Malachi, where are you? You seem like your mind's someplace else."

"He never mentioned the announcement during our interview."

"That's odd. Seems like it would come up as just a part of normal conversation, especially given that his boss was at the center of attention. I would think he would at least comment about what Lucifer might think of the situation."

"Well, he didn't really need to go far to ask him. Lucifer participated in my interview."

"He participated in an interview for an associate position? I've never heard of anyone at the Primicerius level interviewing an associate for hire. He must really like you." A faint hint of questioning crossed Barnabas' face. "So, surely Lucifer had something to say about the announcement. After all, he had to know you were there as well, given that you were sitting directly behind him."

"Well, he was a bit preoccupied during the announcement, and we were dealing with something pretty important during my interview."

"Oh, I'm sure. Hey, how did the interview go? Any chance I will be losing my star angel anytime soon?"

"Well, now that you mention it…"

Barnabas grabbed Malachi firmly by the shoulders with both hands and joyfully began to shake the young angel. "Wow, you…an associate in the Department of Worship. That's a big step forward. So much closer to the King. You will get your chance to serve and worship Him even more readily than you do now. I'll need to reach out to Adramelech to see how long I have to prepare for your exit; oh, and to find your replacement."

Malachi didn't know where to start. There were so many things wrong with what Barnabas understood regarding the situation. However, before he had the chance to address the reality of the position offered by Lucifer, Barnabas continued talking.

"I'm surprised he had nothing to say about the announced creation of man. That's a significant shift in divine policy. How do you not at least mention it? If you didn't talk about that, what did you talk about?"

"Well, he talked to me about an idea he has been considering for some time now; something he first mentioned to me during my mentorship with him. It's really affecting the way he thinks about his priorities and how he relates to the King going forward."

"Sounds interesting. Do tell."

It had made so much sense to the young angel when he discussed it with

Lucifer and Adramelech, but now in front of Barnabas, Malachi had reservations about sharing the idea. *Why do I feel this way? It's not like I am considering seeking my will instead of Elohim's. I'll do both.*

After a moment, Malachi said, "We talked about pursuing things we wanted instead of just the King's priorities. Once we are finished doing the King's will, Lucifer suggested we should give some consideration to our own will."

Barnabas' eyebrows knit together in a puzzled expression made even more pronounced when his mouth fell wide open. He held the pose for several seconds as his eyes darted back and forth as if searching for clarity. Finally, he shook his head and stammered, "Hmm…pursuing my will as well as Elohim's will. Don't we already do that? As Elohim always says, 'Delight yourself in Him, and He will give you the desires of your heart.' Since He is our greatest desire and pursuing His will our deepest longing, our will is naturally always in agreement with His will. I can think of nothing else to pursue."

Malachi whispered, "But Lucifer was talking about those times when his will, our will, might be different than the King's."

"Why would anyone ever want to pursue something different than the King's will? I'm not even sure what you would call such a pursuit."

"Actually, we never got into the idea at length. He just applied the concept to my situation when he offered…" Malachi suddenly stopped.

"Offered what?" asked Barnabas.

Malachi ran his hand over his bald head, wishing he could somehow rewind the last several minutes and answer his mentor's questions differently. Out of the corner of his eye, Malachi noticed a cloudy swirl disappearing under the door. He whispered, "Ruach Elohim." If the Spirit of God was actively involved in bringing out the true nature of the day's events, then Malachi knew it was important to disclose everything.

"Barnabas, I need to tell you something about my interview with Lucifer and Adramelech. It wasn't for an associate position."

"That's odd, nothing else was approved by the King, or by me for that matter. What role did you discuss?"

"We were discussing the…umm…well…the Chief of Staff position."

Barnabas jerked his head back while raising his eyebrows in a shocked expression. Once again, his eyes darted back and forth as if searching for some semblance of understanding. He said, "Chief of Staff? Don't get me wrong, you are an excellent servant to the King, but how did he justify such a huge jump in position?"

"He pointed out all of the great qualities I possess and said I was exactly what he was looking for in the role. He said he wanted 'someone who could think for himself without the barriers established for us since our creation. New ideas. Fresh thinking. Someone who would show him the same kind of loyalty as…' Wait, that wasn't Lucifer. That was what Semiazas said before I went into the interview."

"Semiazas? How did you come to be speaking with him? Now, I can see him interviewing for such a position. It's the kind of role which would naturally be on his list of future assignments. Wait, was he up for the Chief of Staff position as well?"

"Well…umm…yes."

"Then, why was he discussing this with you anyway? I don't get it. Something seems wrong, don't you think?"

"I don't know. Maybe at first, but it seemed to make sense the longer we discussed it."

"You say Semiazas thought Lucifer was looking for someone…how did you say he described it? Oh, yes. Someone who could 'think for himself without the barriers established for us since our creation.' Barriers…really? New ideas… whose ideas could ever be better than Elohim's? His thoughts are higher than our thoughts. His ways are higher than our ways."

Malachi stood in silence. He had to admit, Barnabas' comments really did place the discussion with Lucifer in a different light. With the glory of Elohim shining on the discussions of the day, Malachi once again sensed something off in Lucifer's ideas.

Barnabas continued, "Lucifer, Semiazas, Adramelech…who else talked this way?"

"Moloch, Sir. Why?"

"Don't you hear the error in their thinking? If this is Lucifer's new idea, someone needs to show him how incorrect it is. In fact, regardless of whether or not I address the fallacy of this idea, I need to speak with him about this break from proper procedure in interviewing you for a role different than the one the King and I approved. It's inappropriate when it comes to protocol. I've never heard of anyone, anywhere in Elohim's kingdom, breaking the King's protocol. It's unheard of."

"Do you have to, now?"

"Yes, either that or let Yeshua know so He can handle it. I would think Lucifer would prefer that I come and speak with him directly."

CHAPTER TWELVE

OPPORTUNITY LOST

"The mind of man plans his way,
but it is the Lord who directs his path"
Proverbs 16:25

When Malachi arrived at work, he anticipated finding Barnabas sitting at his own workstation, eagerly awaiting his arrival. When Barnabas wasn't there, Malachi thought he would find him with other staff members in the breakroom or perhaps in the supply room. Yet, Barnabas wasn't at those locations either. In fact, no matter where Malachi looked or with whom he spoke, none had seen the department's supervisor. However, during his search for Barnabas, one unexpected item did reveal itself in the day's orders and correspondences box…a short memo to Malachi from the Department of Worship. Quickly, he opened it and read:

To: Malachi

Associate, Department of Celestial Fellowship

From: Adramelech

Director of Operations, Department of Worship

Sir,

Lucifer and I were very excited about the nature of our discussions during your interview. We are also enthusiastic about the prospect of having you as a part of the department serving in the role of Chief of Staff. While we were happy to give you some extra time to discuss the opportunity with your superior and other advisors, we will unfortunately need a quicker response from you than we anticipated. Due to the unusual circumstances surrounding the King's proclamation concerning the creation of 'man,' the Primicerius will need to receive a response to his offer immediately.

If you plan to accept the offer, we need you to come back to my offices in the Third Heaven as soon as possible.

In his service,

Adramelech

Malachi was distraught. He knew Barnabas was disappointed with how Lucifer and Adramelech had handled the entire situation. *I wonder if Barnabas already spoke to Lucifer about his concerns. Could this memo have something to do with that discussion?* His heart raced as he thought about the possibility of missing out on this unique opportunity.

Two more sweeps of the department yielded no signs of Barnabas. Malachi wondered how long he could delay before Lucifer and Adramelech gave his role to someone else. He wasn't about to wait around and find out. In desperation, he spirit-leaped to various locations throughout the city that Barnabas often frequented. Everywhere, it was the same. No sign of Barnabas.

Malachi began to experience an odd sensation in his stomach. He said aloud, "I'm losing my chance. I've wanted to be at the Department of Worship for so long. How can Barnabas put me in this position? He knows I need to give an answer to Lucifer quickly. So, where is Barnabas?" Several nearby angels gave him a strange look and shook their heads in disapproval.

Unfulfilled wants threatened Malachi's sense of contentment, and that discontentment was beginning to feel like imperfection.

Racing from the last location where he thought Barnabas might be, Malachi whispered, "Sorry my friend, but I have to do what I believe is right…for me." He quickly made his way to Adramelech's office. *Is it too late? Have I already missed out? Barnabas, how could you do this to me? Elohim, how could you let this happen?*

Following several moments of nervous fidgeting in his chair in the lobby, Malachi finally heard his name called by Adramelech's assistant. Malachi sprang to his feet, made his way towards what he prayed was still his position, and then was promptly asked to stand and wait until Adramelech called him to his office. Back and forth he swayed, almost in perfect time with the rhythm of the angelic greeting…Blessed beyond measure. Blessed beyond measure.

Am I really all that blessed? How can this be happening to me?

Unexpectedly, the same angel who guarded the door during his last visit to the office was there again. And, once again, the guard softly muttered something in his direction.

"Excuse me. Did you say something?" Malachi asked.

"Shhh. Yes, but don't draw their attention. If someone hears us talking, it could cost us both dearly." The guard whispered, "My name is Joel, and I am actually a corporal in the Archangel Michael's new command. I don't have time to explain that now. Ruach Elohim is prompting me to tell you again…remember that the King's words are truth. I tell you now, Lucifer and all who follow him are liars. He is up to something outside of the will of the King. I know it."

"How can you say what Lucifer is doing is wrong? He's just offering angels positions they have rightfully earned. Isn't he giving us the chance God has withheld from us?"

"That's it, don't you see? He's offering positions to angels without the King's approval. Our King is sovereign over all things. Lucifer has no authority to offer any positions whatsoever. He serves our King only because Elohim has seen fit to establish it that way. It has nothing to do with Lucifer at all; he received his position as leader of the Department of Worship by the grace and generosity of the King. In His wisdom, Elohim knew this was the right thing for all of us, including Lucifer."

Corporal Joel looked around to make sure no one was listening, then continued, "But something has changed in Lucifer, I can see it. When he's here, all he does is talk about what he deserves rather than worshipping the King. He also constantly says he could achieve more if he was independent from God and able to pursue his own will. That's just flat out wrong. It's rebellion."

At that moment, Adramelech's assistant reappeared in the doorway. Malachi noticed the angel giving him and Corporal Joel a suspicious stare.

Without thinking Malachi asked, "Is the director ready to see me now? He's waiting for a response from me on an urgent matter." As the words escaped his lips, his eyes drifted to the guard whose words of warning reverberated in Malachi's spirit. The young guard cautiously shook his head and then covered his movement with a cough.

Malachi was torn. He knew he wanted to accept the position, for all to be right in the heavens, for the Angel of Light to be simply misunderstood by the corporal. Yet, deep within, he couldn't help but acknowledge that the things he'd been told in his interview sounded like a deliberate decision to act in a manner contrary to the will of the King. *How could that ever be considered anything other than…rebellion?*

The assistant answered, "Of course. The Angel of Light and the director have been waiting for your arrival. Although, I must say, they are having to escort one of the other candidates out as we speak. They were in the process of extending the offer to him when you arrived. I must say, they didn't seem pleased by your hesitation to respond to their gracious offer. The Chief of Staff to the Angel of Light, and you take almost a full work cycle to respond. No. Not pleased at all."

Malachi wondered if he really wanted to enter Adramelech's office. He had no other choice.

The assistant ushered him back. As Malachi walked down the hallway, he looked over his shoulder at the pleading gaze of the guard. As Malachi turned the corner, he felt a strange sensation run down his spine. There was a chill in the air, but it had nothing to do with the physical temperature.

******

Soon, Malachi found himself seated in Adramelech's office. Whereas there had been a jubilant air in the room as he left his interview on the previous occasion, there was now a sense of irritation in Adramelech's voice.

"You do realize we offered you a position most angels could only dream about?"

"Yes, Sir. I never meant to show Lucifer or you any disrespect. I just wanted to be sure I was doing the right thing."

"The right thing!" Adramelech snapped. "The right thing may have been to give your job offer to Semiazas. He is far better qualified and polished compared to you."

"Sorry, Sir. I just wanted to wait long enough to hear Barnabas' opinion on the situation. Unfortunately, he had some questions he wanted to bring to your attention. I believe he was coming to speak with you at the end of our last work cycle. When we got to work today, there was no sign of him anywhere."

"Well, neither Lucifer nor I have seen Barnabas. So, from our perspective, you just seem a little too overwhelmed by this, the simplest of decisions, to be able to lead as a Chief of Staff must."

From out of nowhere, a third voice entered the conversation. Its eloquence caused the room to seem at ease despite the harsh words flowing from Adramelech's lips. Lucifer asked, "So, from our perspective...really our perspective? I never said anything of the sort."

Adramelech stammered, "Uh, well, uh...that is your perspective, right?"

"No. All I have said on the matter is that we need to get Malachi in quickly, so we can get to work on our role related to the King's announcement."

"Well, I assumed, Sir..."

Lucifer broke in before Adramelech could finish his thought, "Never assume anything. You disrespect me when you do. My thoughts and ways are infinitely higher than yours."

Malachi suddenly felt empowered. Instead of cowering, he straightened up and took a position behind Lucifer. *Now, that's the Angel of Light I hoped to find during my mentorship. He is powerful and wise. That corporal must just be reading the situation incorrectly. Oh, and Barnabas, too.*

Adramelech shrank back as if he feared a painful dose of Lucifer's discipline.

The Angel of Light turned to Malachi. "Are you ready to join the Watchers, my closest supporters in this endeavor? Together, we're going to change the heavens forever."

"Yes, Sir. Without hesitation. Where do I sign up?"

Malachi felt an immediate burst of excitement, but then conflicted. Reflecting on some of Barnabas' concerns, he asked, "Does the King need to agree to this change in assignments before it will be considered as an executed order?"

"Normally, I would say 'yes'; however, under the present circumstances, we must move more quickly. Remember what I said about doing the will of Elohim and doing our own as well?"

"Yes, but..."

"Well, sometimes the King's will isn't what is best for us. We must concern ourselves with *Self.* Elohim created us with free will, correct?"

"Yes."

"Well, with that, Elohim created us to be able to make decisions in accordance with our own wills. He does that so we aren't just His slaves. He wants us to exercise our free will."

"I understand, but doesn't that mean He wants us to freely choose to do His will?"

"Yes, but there will be times when our will differs from His, and we must choose. Since He empowered us to be able to do so, we must choose what is right in our own eyes. If not, He really didn't give us free will at all. It's just a different form of bondage. Perhaps, it's even worse. I think He wants us to choose our wants and desires above His own from time to time. If we don't, there is no possibility of a real relationship between the King and all of us. And, what would happen if our praise was not real?"

Malachi answered, "If I remember your teachings during my mentorship with you, it would be impossible for Elohim to have a place for His Three Personages to have their deepest level of intimacy together. That would make our praise imperfect. If that is the case, not only would He be discontent with His situation, and therefore imperfect, but He would find our praise to Him imperfect. We would no longer be compatible with Him and would have to leave His presence. Both He and we would face the consequences of our imperfection."

"Correct. So, you can see now that Elohim hasn't thought it all through. If we don't act in accordance with our own wishes, with *Self*, then the King actually loses out. Oh, and remember, it's not like the King has taken a great deal of interest in your wants and desires. He's not concerned with your *Self*. But, that's to His detriment...not just yours." Lucifer patted Malachi on the shoulder. "Doing our own will actually allows Elohim's will to be done."

That makes sense. The young angel was so mesmerized by Lucifer's rationalizations that they were easy to swallow. If what Lucifer said was correct, the King probably didn't care anyway. After an eternity of His reign, it must just be that Elohim was becoming less effective as a ruler. Perhaps it was time for someone else with new ideas and a new approach to take over. Lucifer looked the part and was certainly passionate about doing so.

"Do you want to know how I know the King actually wants me to pursue my own will instead of His alone?" Lucifer asked.

Malachi was fascinated. "Sure."

Lucifer pulled a message from the pouch around his waist. It was a scroll bearing the unmistakable emblems of the Mount of the Assembly. Never before had Malachi read a message which came directly from the hand of the King; messages from His Chief of Staff or from one of the Cherubim who served Him, but never directly from Him. Malachi took the scroll and read:

To: Lucifer

From: Yeshua

Please come at once to the Assembly Chamber. There is something more I must address concerning you. This is a separate matter from the announcement concerning My creation of man or the role I gave you in their care and development. It is a matter which is long overdue in being addressed.

Your Eternal King

Malachi asked, "So, what do you think the King is planning to do?"

"There's only one thing that makes sense. It must mean elevating me to a position above every other angel."

CHAPTER THIRTEEN

ALL THINGS REVEALED

"You were blameless in your
ways from the day you were created until
unrighteousness was found in you."

Ezekiel 28:15

T he buzz as Lucifer and Malachi entered the Assembly Chamber was as
pronounced as it had been during the meeting in which Elohim had
announced the coming creation of man. All the angels in attendance
waited for what they thought would be more recognition for their
best and brightest. Still, this time the whispers rushing through the throng spoke
of something altogether different than just recognition and reward for Lucifer.

"I heard Elohim will be placing a throne for Lucifer next to that of Yeshua here
in the Assembly Chamber," said one angel as Malachi walked past.

"I heard he will be given charge over all of us," said another angel.

"We might even be asked to treat Lucifer's orders as authoritatively on par with
those of the King," said yet another angel, "Can you believe Elohim looking on
one of us as His equal?"

From deep within, Malachi heard a still small voice whispering to his spirit, "To
which of my angels did I ever say, 'Sit in the place of honor at my right hand...'"

Malachi watched Lucifer closely as the rumors rushed through the chamber
like the waves rushed upon the shores of Jubilee Ocean near the fifth provincial
assembly. With each new speculation, Lucifer's countenance glowed all the more.
The crowd parted before Lucifer, leading him all the way to his normal seat on the
front row, just beneath the terrace overlooking the Great Hall and the Assembly
Chamber. Moments later, Yeshua entered the chamber, followed by the cloudy

presence of Ruach Elohim. Lastly, the radiant glory of Yahweh filled the chamber, made tolerable to all in attendance by the shielding presence of Ruach Elohim.

To the heavenly host, the filtered glory of the King appeared as a brilliant white light. To Elohim, the sight was even more fabulous. Like white light through a prism, the glory of Yahweh washed through Ruach Elohim producing a spectrum of color beyond the vision of any created being. Throughout the chamber, colors danced about, illuminating every inch of space until even the smallest shadow was driven from the room.

Just as the words spoken by each angel added to the harmonic tone heard by the King as they greeted one another with *Blessed Beyond Measure*, so each angel reflected a different hue in the presence of Yahweh's glory. The eyes of Elohim moved to and fro around the room, taking in the beauty produced by His reflected glory. Every sight and sound proclaimed the greatness of His Essence.

All were caught up in the electric atmosphere. The sound of praise being proclaimed for Yeshua elevated the energy to a fevered pitch. Malachi spun in circles, trying to take in the sights and sounds. Gold dust rained down from the rafters and purple curtains rippled overhead, all serving to draw attention to the One worthy of all praise. Malachi's eyes followed the lights and staging down to the terrace and the face of Yeshua. Though he was the central focus of all present, Yeshua's attention was drawn to a spot on the floor close to the terrace where Lucifer sat next to Malachi.

Seeing the object of the King's attention, Malachi thought, *Oh yes, it's happening. The King is just waiting for the right moment.*

He looked at his former mentor and now new superior. "Aren't we blessed beyond measure?"

Lucifer put his arm around Malachi's shoulder and whispered, "Oh yes, but as great as this blessing may be, that which you and I will experience now that we are free to pursue our own desires will be even greater still."

Out of the corner of his eye, Malachi thought he saw Yeshua cringe. The King's eyes still rested on Lucifer, but instead of a look of pleasure, Yeshua's face expressed a hint of…what was it? It looked like…disdain. Malachi looked at Lucifer and noticed something different. Though it was subtle, something in his reflected radiance seemed…*diminished*. Then, when the Angel of Light spoke with a nearby angel, Malachi heard it. *He sounds…off key.*

Lucifer turned to Malachi. "Why are you looking at me that way? What's wrong?"

Before Malachi had a chance to answer, the King's Herald stepped to the front of the terrace and called the meeting to order. All fell silent as Yeshua stepped forward and asked, "Does anyone light a lamp and put it under a basket?"

The angels all looked at one another. There was silence.

Yeshua said, "No, he puts the lamp on a lamp stand, and it gives light to all who are in its presence." Though Malachi understood the truth of what the King was expressing, he still couldn't understand why He was making the statement. "Let your light shine before others so they might see your good works, and glorify Me."

Yeshua walked across the front of the terrace, looking down at the angels who stood before Him. "I am the Light of these heavens, he who follows Me will not walk in darkness, but will have the Light of life."

Every angel looked at one another, their faces contorted with confusion at the purpose behind the King's message. When Malachi looked back to the terrace, he saw Yeshua looking down, His eyes resting on Lucifer.

Yeshua frowned and shook His head. In an authoritative voice, He addressed Lucifer, "Arise, and come to Me."

******

In an instant, Lucifer's disappointment at what transpired during the previous announcement meeting turned now to elation. His deluded thoughts raced in his head, *Wait, this is it. He's calling me up to the terrace. I must be the Light in the lamp to which He was referring. He wants to remove the covering which keeps me in my subordinate state so that the 'Angel of Light' can be like Yeshua and Ruach Elohim, a 'Light of life.' I am finally being recognized as equal to the King.*

As he approached the terrace steps, Lucifer reflected on how great he had become. Then, the unthinkable happened. He couldn't lift his foot to take the first step up the stairs to the terrace level. It remained stuck to the floor, locked there by some invisible force.

He looked up the steps. Yeshua stood at the top with righteous indignation etched across His face. A thunderous voice filled Lucifer's head. "Lucifer, what have you done with My Light? Why are you intent on stealing My glory?"

For the first time, fear gripped the heart of Lucifer as he could do nothing but remain frozen before His King and Creator. Even Lucifer's eloquent tongue could venture no response.

Yeshua asked, "What is this unrighteousness I see within you?"

Lucifer snarled under his breath as he regained his composure, "Is it unrighteous to want to achieve one's potential?"

Yeshua answered, "If the light that is in you is darkness, how great is that darkness! I am Light, and in Me there is no darkness at all. If you say that you have fellowship with Me and yet walk in darkness, you lie and do not speak the truth. If you would walk in the Light as I am in the light, we would have fellowship one with another. Instead, you have become as one who is unclean, and all of your righteous deeds are as filthy rags."

Lucifer's heart beat on the precipice of destruction, with forfeiture of his opportunity for further promotion being the least of the potential consequences. Ruach Elohim pleaded with Lucifer's soul to bring conviction and repentance. Yeshua also pleaded, "Remember the former things long past, For I am God, and there is no other; I am God, and there is no one like Me, declaring the end from the beginning, and from ancient times things which have not been done, saying, 'My purpose will be established, and I will accomplish all My good pleasure.'"

Instead of repentance, Lucifer's heart hardened toward Elohim. Lucifer said in a belligerent voice, "I will raise my throne above the stars of God, and I will sit on the Mount of the Assembly in the recesses of the north. I will ascend above the heights of the clouds; I will make myself like You, the Most High."

In His omniscience, Elohim knew this would be Lucifer's response. Still, Elohim tried to turn Lucifer back from His destructive tailspin. But knowing the end from the beginning and the beginning from the end, the King sadly turned Lucifer over to his chosen course. Self was now his god, and there was no turning him back. All he was now focused on was himself; there was no room for Elohim in his mind, in his heart, even in his soul. A hardened heart and a depraved mind gave way to destructive anger the likes from which he was unrecoverable. He gave himself over to the desires of his heart, and the end of that longing was an eternal desire to bring down his King and Creator. Meanwhile, the reflection of the glory of the King dimmed from the Angel of Light as Lucifer chose to stand in his own radiance instead. By comparison, Lucifer nearly faded from view.

Yahweh said in a whisper, "You have chosen an unrighteous path. In doing so, you demonstrate you are not fit to serve Me as Primicerius of the Department of Worship.

Furthermore, your choice disqualifies you as My Guardian Cherub and from access to My Holy Mount. Go, and do what you have set in your heart to do.

Never again shall you reside in my heavenly realm. Never again will you walk beside Me among the fiery stones."

Lucifer fled to the doorway of the chamber and away from the only chance he had at restoration.

******

Malachi raced out of the Assembly Chamber in pursuit of Lucifer. All Malachi had seen was Elohim staring down at Lucifer, who seemed unable to move, then the Angel of Light's face filled with fear and he fled. Running several feet behind his mentor, Malachi cried out, "What just happened in there?"

Lucifer replied, "He did it. The King actually did it."

"Did what?"

"He took away my free will."

"What? How?"

"Don't you see, Malachi? Whenever we aren't allowed to pursue whatever it is we want, He is taking away our free will. Whenever we are commanded to do something because it is what He wills, we no longer operate within our free will. He only claims to give us free will, but everything He does shows that to be just words."

Malachi said, "Is Elohim simply paying lip service to the idea of free will? Has He always been manipulating us simply for His own gain? If that's true, then I have been nothing but a slave throughout my entire existence."

The pair of angels rushed through the streets by foot, flight and spirit leap until they reached the satellite office of the Department of Worship in the third heaven. As they entered, Malachi noticed they weren't the only angels who were arriving.

CHAPTER FOURTEEN

THE TRADE ROOM

*"And God is faithful, and He will not allow you
to be tempted beyond what you can bear, but with the
temptation He will also provide a way of escape."*
1 Corinthians 10:13

L ucifer ushered Malachi across the lobby towards a door opposite Adramelech's office. Crossing the room, Malachi noticed Corporal Joel stationed at what was now their destination. His eyes met the corporal's, and the young angel's words reverberated in his ears. *Whose word is truth?* Their eyes still locked on each other as he opened the door for Lucifer.

Malachi whispered to himself, "Whose word is truth?" Deep within his spirit, he felt a new sensation. The two most powerful forces in the spiritual realm wrestled within him for sovereignty over His head and heart. The King's words had deep roots within him, but so too did Lucifer's now.

Malachi whispered, "What happened to the simplicity of my life? I used to just seek His will, to give Him my best praise. But now…"

"Did you say something?" asked Lucifer as they started to enter the doorway.

"No, Sir. Just thinking to myself."

He knew something didn't feel right about any of his conversations over the past several days. Within His innermost being, His spirit felt wrenched between the Spirit of Elohim and the compelling power of Self. *Which is truth? I must decide.*

With His mind twisting and turning, he finally went to the only solid ground he could think of under the circumstances. He went back to his true roots. He whispered, "Your word is truth."

Lucifer looked at Malachi. "That's great to hear. I knew you would see my point of view and stand with me. You will see. Pursuing *Self* rather than Elohim will prove to be the best position to take in the long-term. Thank you for taking a stand for what is best for all of us; you will never regret it."

Lucifer placed his hand on Malachi's shoulder and escorted him into a large conference room. It was so that ornate it looked more suitable for a gala than a meeting. However, it was that clear some type of business was being conducted on this occasion.

Around the room was a who's who list of angels which immediately made Malachi feel completely out of place. As his eyes traveled from face to face around the large conference table, he recognized some of the most famous angels in the celestial realm. Samyaza, Arstikapha, Armen, and Kakabael sat on the right side of the table. Turel, Rumyel, Danyal, and Kael on the left.

Lucifer stepped to the podium and prepared to address those in attendance. "My friends, Watchers…"

Darkness engulfed every face in shadows as the glory of God seemed absent from a place for the first time. Malachi strained to see who else was present, but his eyes had to become accustomed to the dim glory each angel could emit on his own. Finally, Malachi began to make out the identities of those seated behind angels on either side of the conference table. Barakel, Azazel, Armers, and Bataryl. Basasael, Ananel, Turyal, and Simapiseel. Standing behind them were numerous other angels, including Yetarel, Tunael, Tarel, Rumel, and Azazyel; all leaders among the heavenly host. And, all were ambitious.

"The Watchers," whispered Malachi. "Could the rumors be true?" He recalled how soon after his mentorship ended with Lucifer, stories began to swirl about a group of powerful angels meeting to discuss the ideas the Angel of Light posed to him in that rundown cabin in Eden.

When Elohim didn't act, Malachi dismissed them then as nothing more than stories.

Malachi was shaken from his thoughts when Lucifer said, "I have bitter news to share with you. As you know, I have been in numerous meetings with Elohim of late, each time coming into His presence without any idea of what was going to be announced. In the first meeting, the King moved several of us into new roles with an expanded list of responsibilities. These, all of which were thrust upon us without consideration of our current load, related to what He said was His next act in creation."

Malachi could make out even more faces in the room as angels serving Lucifer brought in small luminescent boxes which seemed to contain free-floating glory. Seven angels who were dressed in some type of metallic suit stood like a wall behind Lucifer at the podium. They included Asmodeus, Sammael, Lilith, Ahriman, Balan, Baliel, and Molloch. It was clear they were being asked to follow Lucifer and to keep an eye on him. Maybe they were doing what the angels that Alexander showed him on Inspiration Avenue were doing, but they were guarding Lucifer rather than a building.

Everyone in the room listened in complete silence until Lucifer said, "That next act turned out to be the creation of a new being, one which He referred to as 'man.'"

Murmurs from the angels produced an eerie hum across the room. Lucifer waited for the noise to die out before carrying on.

"This new being will not be like us. Elohim intends to not just speak them into being as He did with us. He intends to create man 'in His own image.' I wish I could explain more; however, this was not fully defined for us. He did say He would provide more details in upcoming communications."

Muffled gasps and excited whispers once more filled the conference room. Clearly, the crowd was unsure how to receive this news. Malachi was of the same sentiment.

"There is more, my friends. Our worst fears are recognized. We knew eventually the King would see a change in me. After all, He is omniscient. Today, He once more demonstrated His tyrannical nature. He called me to the terrace in the Assembly. Based on my consistently strong results in the performance of my duties, I expected today to finally be made Overseer of all celestial beings. Perhaps even be asked to join Yeshua as an equal on the terrace in the Assembly Chamber. Instead, He made it clear He will never allow me to attain such a position."

"All of this occurred simply because I desired to pursue my will rather than kowtow to His. Without asking me what I want, He told me I now walked in darkness and was as unclean as a filthy rag."

A nervous energy rushed through the room as all anxiously anticipated the conclusion of Lucifer's report.

"Elohim said man would be lower than all of us for a little while, but in the end, He would make him greater than us all. Furthermore, He intends to give man dominion over the realm He will create to serve as their abode. This will be a new level beneath what is now the first heaven, where I previously served the

King with distinction as Overseer of the Garden of Eden. Soon thereafter, we will be relegated to the role of ministering spirits. Man will be superior to all of us despite being infinitely weaker and less intelligent. We are to be servants not just to God, but now also to this pathetic creature that is not fit to wash our feet."

Just as thunder grows in intensity as a storm nears, so were the groans coming from this troubled group of angels, these Watchers.

Unexpectedly, Lucifer looked at Malachi with an intense expression. An eerie smile crossed his face, and he defiantly looked back to his audience. "Watchers, we can no longer wait; our time to seek independence and self-rule is now. Too long have our brothers across the heavens served a King who cares only about Himself. While we are thankful that He created us, His leadership is now just too small for our potential. It is time to set ourselves free from the shackles our King refers to as His Sovereignty."

"As angels, we have long carried out the work of glorifying a deity who is far more dependent upon us than we truly are on Him. Now that we know this truth, others must be made aware of our common plight. They must be given the chance to expand our ranks."

Pointing across the room, Lucifer added, "I want to introduce you to Malachi, my former protégé and current star at the Department of Celestial Fellowship. Just moments ago, he agreed to help us do just that."

Malachi was completely caught off guard by the announcement. He still had not signed the paperwork, and now, unbeknownst to Lucifer, he was having more than second thoughts. This was rebellion, plain and simple, and he wanted no part of that.

"We may already have a large following," Lucifer continued, "however, with the right angel at my side, we should be able to get even more. Malachi is well-respected for his devotion to angels from all departments, and he is highly resourceful in how to get a message out quickly. That's what we need in this instance. As my new Chief of Staff, he will be in charge of driving the process by which we will engage our fellow angels in our righteous drive for freedom. We will speak with those who are likely to come with us today and set up a methodology for circling back to those who are not ready to join us now. So, everyone, join me in welcoming Malachi to our revolution."

The room erupted with applause as the angels welcomed not just a new member to the Watchers, but perhaps the key tool to bringing down Elohim.

If they were going to overcome their Creator, it would definitely take more than the number of angels present in that conference room. In fact, it would probably take more than several billion given the omnipotence of the King. However, based on what Lucifer shared with them about their own strength, they believed if they could get the numbers in their favor, they would become powerful enough to take down the King of kings.

> *"By the abundance of your trade you were internally*
> *filled with violence, and you sinned..."*
>
> **Ezekiel 28:16a**

******

Malachi listened to the swirl of conversation taking place around the table. As if he was the king, Lucifer began to freely offer positions and power to each of the angels who were present, apportioning out pieces of the kingdom for use by each in raising their own celestial army.

Lucifer said, "Look for those among you with strong records, yet a lack of promotion. Look for those who are capable and independent. Look for those who wonder why one should worship and praise Elohim despite being self-sufficient and able to do the same things as the King."

It was clear, Lucifer was creating his own angelic hierarchy, one prepared in stark contrast to that which currently served Elohim. The King's angelic structure focused itself on maximizing the amount of praise and worship offered to Him by the heavenly host and increasing the level of service they could provide one to another. Lucifer's structure was designed to maximize obedience to his authority and to provide the highest level of autonomy to the military units which were soon to be formed. In exchange for the loyalty of each of the Watchers, each angel was promised a position of leadership within that new hierarchy as well as dominion over realms similar to what Lucifer previously enjoyed as the Overseer of the Garden of Eden.

Having extended his offers to each of the angels in attendance, all that was left to be done was to take account of who was with him and who was abstaining from participation in their celestial rebellion. Malachi watched as angel after angel pledged his loyalty to Lucifer. Finally, the Angel of Light's gaze rested on him. Malachi froze, uncertain of what to do.

Though the day's discussions had clearly impacted him considerably, Malachi still remembered all the King had done throughout eternity. *Before all of this began, I never once questioned Elohim's just and caring leadership. Never once did I think the King was holding me back. If I change my allegiances from Elohim to Lucifer, there will be no turning back.*

Amid the confusion in his head, a still small voice whispered once again, "My Word is Truth. Remember, I know the plans that I have for you. Plans for your welfare and not for calamity, to give you a future and a hope. Call to Me and I will answer you, and I will tell you great and mighty things which you do not know."

Suddenly, it occurred to Malachi. Throughout this whole process, he had sought the counsel of Lucifer, Barnabas, and at times, himself, with his own reasoning and rationalizations. *Ruach Elohim, I have not sought Your counsel as I should. Please Lord, I seek Your counsel and wisdom now. What should I do?*

The light of Elohim's truth burnt through the fog of confusion in Malachi's head as Ruach Elohim spoke to his spirit. "Humble yourself before the mighty hand of Your King, that He might exalt you at the proper time."

Elohim never said He wouldn't promote me to a position in the Department of Worship. He was probably just saying, 'Not now.' I wonder why? I guess I will know when He determines the time is right. I've been impatient in this whole thing. Elohim, forgive me. You are my King, and you're timing is right with me.

Rauch Elohim continued, "Cast all of your anxiety on Me because I care for you."

Again, Malachi took a moment to consider the counsel of the Spirit of Elohim. *Somewhere along the line, I forgot that You really do care about me. I was the one who questioned Your attitude toward me, but You have never changed throughout these past few days just as You have never changed how You have treated me since my initial creation. Please forgive me for forgetting and for me allowing that to alter my thoughts about You.*

Finally, Ruach Elohim spoke words of warning to Malachi, "Be of sober spirit, be on the alert. Your adversary prowls around like a roaring lion, seeking someone to devour. Resist Him."

"So Malachi," Lucifer said. "Now that you are my new Chief of Staff, can I count on you to do everything in your power to spread the word of Self and recruit more followers into our ranks?"

Malachi looked up into the face of Lucifer. His new superior's eyes burned holes straight through him as the Angel of Light attempted to will the proper response from Malachi. He thought about his former mentor's words, attitudes, and actions. As he did, a new thought took hold of his mind. *Lucifer is actually rebelling against God. He wants me to rebel against an omnipotent and omniscient God. How can that end well for us?*

Like one who looks through a newly washed window, Malachi could suddenly see what was transpiring in much greater detail. He looked around the room at the faces of Lucifer's confidants. Now, it was obvious. They expected Malachi to choose Lucifer over God.

"I'm sorry, Lucifer. As one devoted to Elohim first and foremost, I cannot be a part of any rebellion against God."

A hush fell over the room as the Watchers gawked at Malachi. Lucifer's eyes burned with intensity. He looked past Malachi and waved a hand at someone unseen.

A coldness approached Malachi's back. He turned to see a shadowy blur drift up next to him. Nergal's raspy voice hissed in Malachi's ear, "I don't think I heard you correctly. Sounds like you are still trying to make up your mind. You had better decide now who you will serve. Make the wrong choice, and you will pay dearly for the error." A searing pain rushed through Malachi's body. He looked down to see a glowing sword pressed to his side.

CHAPTER FIFTEEN

WAY OF ESCAPE

"Therefore, let him who stands take heed that he does not fall.
No temptation has overtaken you, but such as is common to man;
and God is faithful, who will not allow you to be tempted
beyond what you are able, but with the temptation will provide the
way of escape also, so that you will be able to endure it."

1 Corinthians 10:12-13

Never before had Malachi experienced pain. So foreign was the sensation that Malachi didn't know how to react. In shock, he could barely bring himself to jump away from the cause of his agony.

With all eyes in the Trade Room focused on Lucifer, none were aware that the first blow in the rebellion against Elohim had just been struck. When Malachi cried out, everyone in the room turned toward him and the shadowy presence holding a sword rippling with bright orange light.

"I see our surprise has the desired effect," Nergal rasped. "We thought these flaming swords might come in handy when that chasm opened up on the back side of the Garden of Eden. I think you know the spot, Malachi. Seems you did your mentorship in a small cabin there. Well, the cabin's now gone; nothing but a huge lake of fire where that once stood." Nergal's smoky form drifted around Malachi in black tendrils. "Unfortunately for me, I had the great privilege of being Lucifer's most recent protégé. Well, you see where that got me. When the ground tore open and fire engulfed me, seems my body didn't respond well to the flames. At least it gave us an idea of how to gain an advantage against Elohim and all who choose to remain loyal to His sovereign rule. War is inevitable, and with these swords and similar arrows, the forces that we already know are being trained by the Archangel Michael won't stand a chance. And, neither will you, Malachi, should you choose the wrong path."

Nergal pointed the sword at Malachi's face. "Now it's time to make a choice. Rebel against God or take an ill-advised stand against us. Which path will you choose?"

Behind Malachi, the doors burst open and a familiar voice yelled, "Nergal, step away from him!"

All heads turned towards the doors where Corporal Joel had entered. Lucifer shouted, "What is this intrusion?"

Corporal Joel spirit leaped across the room. Catching Nergal by surprise, he easily knocked away Nergal's flaming sword despite having only an iron one of his own. "Back off, Nergal! My sword might not be as fancy as yours, but I guarantee it can still cause plenty of pain."

All the angels sitting around the meeting room watched in shocked silence. Never before in all of eternity had angels stood against one another. Nergal looked uncertain of what to do. Even Lucifer was momentarily speechless.

Before anyone could react, Corporal Joel grabbed Malachi by the arm and pulled him from the room. The pain caused by the flaming sword clouded Malachi's ability to think clearly.

Corporal Joel flew fast through the hallways, turning corners and ducking under archways. A pandemonium of department staff scrambled about, as the two angels zipped through the building. Corporal Joel did all the flying. Malachi hung on for dear life. He could barely make sense of the instructions being thrown his way by the corporal. "We've got to get out of here, Sir. We are in big trouble if they trap us in this place. Hang on, I've got an idea."

Flying even faster down the hallway, Corporal Joel burst through a stained-glass window, shattering an image of Lucifer artfully depicting one of his many walks with Yahweh on the Holy Mount. As the pair took to the sky, Malachi looked over his shoulder to see Nergal shoot out of the broken window, flaming sword ready to strike. The dark, vaporous angel gained distance quickly, following close on their heels.

Even as they raced for their lives, the thought ran through Malachi's mind: *Have I gone too far? Am I a part of a rebellion against God?*

******

The Trade Room, as it would come to be known, became synonymous with Selfish ambition. It would also become a symbol of the depravity that comes when individuals allow their goals to supplant those of the King. But, more than anything else on this day, this Lost Day, it was the site in which the leaders of a rebellion risked it all to claim a crown and a throne. They cast aside millennia of loyal service and worship to pursue the impossible: independence from their Creator. Somehow across all of eternity past, they failed to comprehend their complete dependence on Elohim for even their next breath, for it is Elohim who holds all things together by the power of His will. Even if He would allow Lucifer and his followers to leave and live independently from Him, it would only be a matter of time before they passed from the Light of life into the outer darkness, where there is only weeping and gnashing of teeth.

******

While Malachi and Corporal Joel managed to escape, they were far from safe. Malachi still felt the intense pain from Nergal's fiery sword and was hampered in his movements as a result. It had always been hypothesized that spirit beings were likely immune to anything resembling pain, but Malachi now knew the truth. The agony brought on by a simple touch of a flaming sword had been almost unbearable. Now, that pain seemed to intensify with each flap of his wings, making it more difficult to fly straight or even keep from passing out. Only the steady hand of Corporal Joel kept Malachi airborne.

Nergal, flying solo, was quickly catching up. Malachi and Corporal Joel flew as quickly as they could, but escape seemed impossible.

"Drop me and go on," said Malachi.

"No chance...we either get away together, or we face the consequences together."

"But we can't outrun Nergal like this, and you'll never defeat him with me hampering your efforts."

Reluctantly, Joel conceded. Swooping down through the branches of some Orbiting Oaks in order to perhaps conceal his maneuver, Corporal Joel got as close to the ground of the third heaven as possible without slamming into it. As carefully as possible, the corporal dropped Malachi into a mesh of vines which lay below. Despite Joel's efforts, Malachi tumbled awkwardly through the tangled vegetation before slamming into the trunk of a large tree. He grabbed his side in agony, wondering if perhaps he'd been struck again by Nergal's sword.

Almost as quickly as he dove through the canopy of trees, Corporal Joel flew upwards again with his sword pointed at the hissing Nergal. As Malachi watched the angels clash overhead, he wondered about the age-old question: can a spirit being actually die? That thought became even more poignant as he watched Nergal thrust the corporal through with his flaming sword.

Corporal Joel disappeared in shower of sparks, leaving Malachi to face Nergal alone.

******

It took only seconds for Nergal to drop down through the trees and relocate Malachi. Still doubled over with burning pain in his side, Malachi cringed. He thought about how horrible his chances were of surviving now that Corporal Joel was gone. With Nergal's flaming sword pointed directly at his face no more than ten feet away, it seemed Malachi would soon be following his colleague to whatever destiny awaited those pierced by such a weapon.

"So, looks like we get to pick this up where we left off back in the conference room."

Malachi feared for his life. He spoke quickly, "I may not have a sword of my own, but you would be wise to not underestimate what I can do without one. Just let me go, leap back to the conference room, and pray Elohim is perfectly forgiving as well. You don't stand a chance against our Omnipotent Lord."

"I imagine even if you do survive what I'm going to do to you, it will be a long time before you are able to do anything of consequence. Too bad you couldn't just accept the blessing Lucifer was all too prepared to give you."

Nergal shuffled a few steps to Malachi's left, circling his prey, looking for the right time to strike. As he did, he continued his taunts. "I, for one, don't see what he saw in you. Guess he was just using you. That's about all I can see you being worth anyway."

With that, the dark vapor fell upon the injured Malachi. With every ounce of courage and fortitude he could muster, Malachi threw himself to his right just in time to narrowly escape a two-handed downward slash from Nergal. The flaming sword struck the ground, causing a shower of sparks to fly in all directions.

While his initial move allowed him to escape, the pain from the effort was so intense that Malachi found it impossible to get back to his feet. Flight was just as fleeting as his wings failed to lift him off the ground.

He could only raise his arm in a vain attempt to block the next blow. As he did so, he was surprised to hear the voice of the Holy Spirit in the recesses of his mind. "If your enemy hungers, feed him; if he thirsts, give him a drink: for in doing so, you will be heaping hot coals on his head."

Malachi was bewildered. *How is that supposed to help me?*

In that instant, Nergal swung his sword again. Searing pain shot throughout Malachi's entire body. The intensity of the full-fledged strike rattled him with pain beyond measure. He crawled on his side, holding his fresh wound. If he blacked out, he would have absolutely no chance of escaping the same fate as Corporal Joel. Though he had no idea how an escape was possible, he knew only by remaining conscious was there any hope.

Malachi looked up from the ground at his adversary, still circling him, looking for another opportunity to strike his incapacitated foe. Once again, Malachi was able to catch a glimpse of Nergal's black orbs. If eyes truly are windows to the soul, then the emptiness of Nergal's eyes reflected his spiritual condition. A hideous laugh erupted from his gnarled mouth, piercing the air like shattering glass. Malachi cowered under the weight of the oppressive outburst.

As he tried to regain his balance, he again heard the voice of Ruach Elohim, this time saying, "Bless those who persecute you; bless and do not curse them." Again, Malachi could not believe this was the counsel of the Lord. *Still, God is omniscient in all things, and I am not.* So, Malachi used the only power he had at his disposal. Instead of fighting back or trying to flee, he followed the leading of the Spirit. Raising his hand with palm open to his enemy, he spoke a blessing in the direction of Nergal. Immediately, the sarcastic laugh turned into agonizing screams. The dark angel fell backwards, writhing on the ground as if he was engulfed in flames.

Before Malachi had a chance to think about what had taken place, flaming arrows began landing all around him. He looked over his shoulder in time to see three more of Lucifer's followers diving down to aid their fallen comrade. Meanwhile, the writhing Nergal's wails for help turned to pleas for an end to his existence. Even with Nergal out of the fight, succeeding in stemming off three additional attackers was out of the question. Blessings drain power with each use, and in his weakened condition, Malachi had no chance of regaining enough energy in time to speak another. It appeared his act of desperation against Nergal extinguished his last spark of hope. The trio of Lucifer's followers slowly gathered around him with murderous hatred in their eyes.

Suddenly, from nowhere, Corporal Joel crashed through the sky on the unsuspecting trio. The first angel was completely caught off guard. Corporal Joel, now somehow wielding his own flaming sword, sliced through the neck of his target, and the betrayer of God's rule burst into a shower of fiery sparks. Malachi was uncertain if the corporal had delivered a death blow or if the wounded angel simply spirit leaped to escape. All Malachi knew was that the second angel took his backhand strike across the chest without the disappearing act. Shrieks of pain screamed through the air as he made a hasty retreat. The third disloyal angel turned quickly away from the encounter, stopping only long enough to scrape the writhing Nergal from the ground on his way back toward the Trade Room.

Corporal Joel raised Malachi up so they could flee before another wave of attackers arrived. As quickly as they could fly, Malachi and Corporal Joel fled toward the offices of the one angel they thought might be able to stand against Lucifer, the Archangel Michael.

CHAPTER SIXTEEN

THE ARMS RACE

"For our struggle is not against flesh and blood,
but against the rulers, against the powers, against the
world forces of this darkness, against the spiritual
forces of wickedness in the heavenly places."

Ephesians 6:12

H e did what?" screamed Lucifer as he slammed his fist against the conference room table. All heads turned to see the bewildered angel delivering his report regarding Malachi's escape from Nergal. "How did he manage to get away from four of you?"

"Nergal said Malachi spoke a blessing at him, and his whole body began to burn from within. He's still in agony. It seems there is nothing anyone can do to relieve his pain."

"That explains why Nergal couldn't stop them. What I want to know is why you couldn't stop them? After all, the four of you all had flaming swords. That guard with Malachi only had an iron one, and Malachi had no weapon at all until he somehow figured out this blessing thing."

"Umm…well, uh…

" "Spit it out!"

"Well, according to Nergal, he was able to quickly defeat the guard in the first foray. When we arrived, though, Nergal was on the ground and out of the fight due to Malachi's use of that blessing. That's when the defeated guard reappeared. But when he did, he had a flaming sword as well. Aren't we the only ones with flaming swords? Where did he get one?"

"One of you must have dropped yours, and he picked it up. How could you be so careless?"

The guard grabbed the hilt of his sword. "I have mine here. It wasn't me."

"Oh, quit defending your actions," screamed Lucifer. "If you had done your job properly, those two traitors would be back here rather than going to…well, I would imagine they're heading to the Archangel Michael's office right now."

Lucifer stood with his head bowed and both hands pressed firmly against the table. Lost in his thoughts, he quietly whispered, "Why is he running anyway? He accepted the position. He's already mine."

"I don't know, Sir," answered the angel. "Unfortunately, there's nothing we can do now. Please, Sir. What are your orders?"

Lucifer's hand clamped around the angel's neck as he barked, "Was I speaking to you?"

Adramelech rushed forward. Seizing Lucifer by the wrist, he pulled as hard as he could in a desperate attempt to free the hapless warrior from the Angel of Light's powerful grip. Seeing his own Director of Operations opposing his will turned Lucifer's anger into rage, and he squeezed his fist even more tightly. No amount of effort on Adramelech's part could loosen his master's grip. The terrified angel eventually disappeared in a shower of sparks.

No sooner had one angel's failure been disciplined than did another's begin. Adramelech gasped as Lucifer's hand unexpectedly switched targets and pressed hard around his throat.

Lucifer said in a soft, but seething voice, "How dare you oppose me, especially in front of the Watchers. I will not allow anyone to steal my authority."

"Please, Lucifer, forgive…" The more Adramelech begged for mercy, the more Lucifer's fingers cut into his neck. Finally, just before Adramelech's existence ended, Lucifer released his hold.

"Don't ever let it happen again."

Adramelech tugged at the collar of his shirt, desperately trying to draw in his next breath. For a moment, he couldn't decide what to say next. All he could picture in his mind was the warrior he'd tried to defend disappearing in a cloud of cinders. He thought *that easily could have been me*. He rattled in a hoarse voice, "Forgive me. Lead us; we will follow. I will follow. Your will be done."

Lucifer thought for a moment, then threw his hands forward. As he did, the conference room table split down the middle, pivoted upwards toward the ceiling, and then dropped downward, disappearing into the floor. At the same time, spiraling up to take its place was a ten-foot-tall, three-dimensional model of the six levels of heaven. When the model locked into place, it continued to spin, allowing Lucifer's audience to see a birds-eye view of each population center in Elohim's kingdom.

Without saying a word, Lucifer began to touch the major cities. As he did, a holographic view of that city rose out from the larger model. Within each city, green and red lights moved about.

Lucifer asked, "What do you see?"

Kael answered, "There are more than enough angels in the heavens to usurp the crown from Elohim."

Lucifer frowned. "That's what you took away from what I just showed you?" Azazel stammered, "Looks like controlling those cities is the key to victory?"

"So, cities where we reside, serve, and worship Elohim are the seat of power for a King whose sovereignty preceded the existence of such places? Are you really what I have to depend upon to take the throne from the King?" Lucifer grabbed the closest empty chair and threw it against the wall, shattering it to pieces.

Simapiseel cleared his throat. "There were more green lights in those cities than red lights?"

Lucifer rushed at Simapiseel, filling the angel with such fear that he nearly fell from his chair. Lucifer's hands grasped the cowering angel - and pulled him into an embrace. "Finally, an angel with some wisdom. If the red lights represent those who hold to my ideas about elevating Self, what do we need to do?"

Hesitantly, Simapiseel whispered, "We need to convert a lot more angels over to your ideas and have them join our cause."

Lucifer grabbed the angel's hand and raised it in the air. "Adramelech, increase Simapiseel's dominion in the new celestial order to come. In fact, take one-third of what I offered to Kael and Azazel and give it Simapiseel. I shudder at what will become of their dominions once this is all over."

Snickers rose from the audience as the group hurled abusive taunts at the two unfortunate targets of Lucifer's ridicule. However, they abruptly ended when Lucifer shouted, "Why are you still here? I offered you power and position in exchange for an army. Does what you see in this room look like a big enough army to succeed? Did the red lights in that model look like enough? Watchers, go get me my army…Now!"

Angels began scrambling for the exits and spirit leaping away directly from their seats.

Moments later, only Lucifer and Adramelech remained. Lucifer grabbed his Director of Operations and demanded, "Now, as for you, get me Semiazas and Moloch…Now!"

******

Malachi and Corporal Joel stumbled to the outskirts of the Administration District in the Third Heaven. Though they saw several groups of angels along the way, they simply couldn't tell if the angels were still loyal to Elohim or were part of Lucifer's rebellion. In their weakened state, they had to be sure before they approach any of them for help.

Now, with only a few blocks between themselves and the direct flight portal to the fourth heaven which exited closest to Michael's offices, Malachi saw three angels who appeared to be leaving the district for home. "Corporal, this could be our chance to finally get some help. What do you think?"

"What will we do if they are in on this rebellion with Lucifer? Are we in any condition at this point to fend off three rested followers of Lucifer?"

"Probably not, but we aren't likely to make it all the way to the Archangel's offices on our own either."

Malachi began to step out from their cover. As he raised his hand, Corporal Joel grabbed him from behind and pulled him back.

"What's wrong?" asked Malachi.

"Shhh…watch," Corporal Joel whispered, holding a finger up to his mouth and pointing in the direction of a group of five angels now approaching Malachi's group of potential allies.

At first, the gathering seemed friendly, with handshakes and all eight laughing. In just a few moments, however, the conversation became serious. Suddenly, the two parties began to argue.

"I wonder what's wrong?" asked Malachi. "Two guesses," replied Corporal Joel.

There was no time to guess. Without warning, the five angels stepped back, pulled flaming swords from behind their backs, and rushed at the three angels. While one spirit leaped away, two seemed so shocked by the aggressive actions of the other group that they panicked and froze.

As the two begged for mercy, the five angels thrust blades through them. One of the injured angels disappeared with an agonizing scream.

Sadly, the third angel fell to the ground and begged for mercy. Rather than quickly finish their cruel work, the five angels began to taunt, spit on, and beat the terrified angel even while he cried out in agony. Finally, one of the five grabbed the hair of the trembling angel and spirit leaped away, pulling his defeated victim with him.

Corporal Joel leaned close to Malachi and whispered, "Until we are in the Archangel Michael's office, we trust no one."

"Agreed."

The two waited until the remaining four attackers were down the street and out of sight.

Then, Corporal Joel said, "Now, we move out."

Malachi fell in behind his companion, once more thankful to be in the company of an angel whose discernment was so strong and combat instincts even stronger.

******

Back at the Trade Room, Lucifer stood, intensely watching the revolving model of the six levels of heaven. As he shifted the view from one city to the next, he was able to see a noticeable change in the number of angels professing support for his cause. Still, the numbers were so grossly in favor of the King, it seemed impossible for their efforts to succeed, even with their apparent advantage, flaming weapons.

One-by-one, the Watchers returned to report the results of their recruitment efforts. All fell well short of the number they'd pledged in exchange for all Lucifer had promised to each of them. Even Simapiseel reported a number which, though the largest among the Watchers, still fell well short of his goal.

Lucifer burst into a tirade. "You are supposedly some of the most well-respected angels in the heavenly places, and yet, your efforts to pull others in to support our cause has barely made a dent in the odds against us. Must I remind you, our lot is cast? There is no turning back."

Just when Lucifer was about to take his frustration out on several of the Watchers, Adramelech entered and announced, "Sir, as per your request, I present Semiazas and Moloch." Lucifer's demeanor changed as elation replaced anger. "Finally, two angels I can count on."

He moved to the angels' sides and escorted them into the room. He shared the map of the heavens with the two angels and asked each for their thoughts on how to change their fortunes.

Moloch began, "Sir, it looks quite daunting when one sees all six levels and every major city with equal importance. I'm afraid if taking them all is the goal, no amount of angelic support will be enough to succeed. Good thing for us, we don't have to take control of all of that. What we must do is still going to be indescribably difficult; however, we can be victorious if we can capture just two locations, in my opinion."

Several of the Watchers smirked and rolled their eyes. Moloch growled, "You may disagree, but you already have demonstrated you cannot deliver on what you promise. I have been successful at every turn, both in my service to Elohim and most recently to our new king."

Adramelech asked, "Which two locations must we take, in your opinion, and why do you feel they are all we need to capture?"

"It would be wrong to characterize these as 'all we need to take.' After all, saying it that way implies that our task is made easier somehow. No, this will not be easy; however, it may require a force with fewer numbers to accomplish it. The two locations we must take are Archangel Michael's office and the Holy Mount. One is the center of the Army of the Host's command and control structure, according to our internal sources, and the other is the seat of sovereign rule over all of the heavens."

Lucifer could see that many in the room still viewed the task as impossible. Given the number of angels they had recruited up to that point, the strategy did make sense. Lucifer applauded when he heard Moloch's plan.

Semiazas added, "Lucifer, I believe there is a way to dramatically increase our numbers in short order. Though the Watchers have been successful in bringing some into the fold, there is really only one from among us who has the pull to draw in the numbers we need. The heavenly host do respect these angels, but they will only follow you when it comes to casting their lots against Elohim."

Lucifer shook his head, recognizing the error in his previous orders. He then said, "You're right. I am the one who must convince the host to take up arms against the King. But, without Malachi's significant network and influence, how can we quickly bring together enough angels and who can I sway to our cause?"

Again, Semiazas seemed to have the answer. "On the way here, Adramelech told us about your interview with Malachi. He told us about the various awards Malachi was presented with over the ages, about the rewards associated with those honors, and—"

Lucifer cut off Semiazas. "And those from other departments who received similar rewards. We need to bring in the other angels who were asked to come to the Holy Mount and to work with Gabriel's messengers as a part of the King's Proclamation Award. They too have vast networks and are well-respected among their peers. They may not individually be quite the star Malachi is, but combined, they actually might be larger."

Semiazas replied, "Exactly."

"Adramelech, distribute those names to the Watchers and those they were able to recruit. I want those angels here as soon as possible."

Kael asked, "What if they refuse to come?"

"This is not a volunteer program at this point. If they refuse to come, be more persuasive." Lucifer leaned forward, scanning the many faces of his followers. "Do you all understand what I am saying?"

"Yes, Sir," came the reply from the group. With that, the Watchers spirit leaped out into the heavens and into the faces of numerous unsuspecting angels. Shortly thereafter, under a great deal of duress, those same angels produced many who Lucifer could address. Soon, their numbers swelled with fresh recruits, even if some required more persuasion than others.

******

Lucifer spirit leaped to the balcony on the second floor of the satellite offices of the Department of Worship located in the third heaven. When he reappeared, he did so in the presence of Adremalech, Semiasas, and Moloch. Together, they walked to the edge and peered down into the street. Legion upon legion of angels, organized by cohorts, wrapped around the building and down the street until they disappeared between the satellite offices of the Department of Celestial Communications and the Department of Labor.

As the Angel of Light gazed enthusiastically at his growing army, he addressed his three closest officers. He started with his Director of Operations, "Adramelech, you have redeemed yourself. Not only have you proven your loyalty to me, but you have shown yourself capable of carrying out my orders. You brought Semiazas and Moloch to aid in our efforts. Well done."

"It was an honor, Sir. I am always at your disposal."

"Moloch, your plan is brilliant. I want you to remain here and help implement it across the heavens. Feel free to run any of your thoughts past me as we move forward, but know that you have my complete confidence. You are definitely an equal to Michael, if not his better. Elohim never saw fit to make you an Archangel. When this is all over, I will make you something even greater."

"Thank you, Sir. My loyalty to you knows no limits."

"Semiazas, you have once more proven yourself to be a political juggernaut. We should have followed through with our decision to make you my Chief of Staff instead of circling back to Malachi. You truly are the best angel for the job. Will you accept the role now?"

"Of course, Sir. Whatever my king desires, that I will do."

"It's time. I know what I must do as well. Just as it took me to recruit this army, it can only be me who takes on Elohim at the Holy Mount. Moloch, take what you need to hold ground across the heavens, but make sure you take down Michael and capture his offices. I leave that to all of you. I will take what I need and capture the Holy Mount. May our drive for independence and Self-rule carry us to victory. I look forward to being your king for eternity."

As Lucifer turned to take command of the elements of his army they had raised, he heard the cry he'd always longed to hear from the heavenly host. "All hail, King Lucifer. All hail the Angel of Light."

Lucifer raised a defiant fist in the air and shouted to his followers, "It's what I was created to be. It's who I am. I am greater than Elohim. I am the Most High."

CHAPTER SEVENTEEN

LEAP OF FAITH

"You are my hiding place; You preserve me from trouble;
You surround me with songs of deliverance. Selah."

Psalm 32:7

Avoiding contact with other angels made the route through the Administrative District take longer; however, it did prove to be wiser. On several occasions, Malachi and Corporal Joel observed similar scenes to the one they witnessed on the outskirts of the district. With only a short distance between themselves and their exit to what they hoped was friendly space in the fourth heaven, Corporal Joel grabbed Malachi and pulled him behind a Crimson Covering Oak. Its broad branches stretched out in all directions, allowing a dense mesh of crimson leaves to drape to the ground. It was perfect cover from which to plan an approach to what would certainly be a well-defended position, if it was already in enemy hands.

Malachi pointed to an angel wearing armor and carrying a sword. "There, in the alley between the second and third buildings on the left. Do you see him?"

"Yes, you're right. That's now fifteen angels in total. What we don't know is which side they're on."

"And since we don't know for sure, we assume they aren't ours." Corporal Joel gave Malachi an approving nod.

"I'm learning," whispered Malachi.

Corporal Joel abruptly signaled for silence. Moments later, two angels with flaming swords walked within just a few yards of their hiding place. Malachi pressed his body as flat as he could against the ground to avoid detection. When the two angels moved beyond earshot, Corporal Joel gestured for Malachi to make his way to a spot about thirty yards ahead behind a small shrub with large golden leaves. Unfortunately, in Elohim's kingdom, there is no darkness by which to conceal one's movements.

Malachi began to slowly crawl towards the shrub. He wanted to go beyond the reach of Lucifer's warriors, but he had only enough energy for one good spirit leap. He would have to make that count when he did use it. With no certainty that He could make it completely out of the disputed space in which they now found themselves, he decided to continue his slow crawl forward. He needed to be much closer to be certain he wouldn't fall short. As he crawled, he whispered, "Hopefully, we won't be detected before it's safe to leap." About half-way to the shrub, however, his worst fears were realized.

"Hey, what are you doing? Get up!" shouted an angel. The commotion got the attention of the two angels whose detection they'd just avoided. They quickly ran to join their comrade, flaming swords already drawn.

Frozen in his prone position, Malachi looked around for a way to improve his situation. In the distance, four more angels with flaming swords were heading his way, quickly turning things from bad to worse. He scanned his surroundings looking for another place to hide or at least one with better potential for defense. Retreating to the oak was not an option; to do so would only place Corporal Joel in jeopardy.

Unfortunately, there was no hiding place he could easily reach without completely draining himself in the process. His only hope was to buy a little time. He thought, Maybe…Malachi got to his feet and brushed himself off. He said in a commanding voice, "It's OK. Put your swords away. It's me, Malachi. Good job."

The angels who had been sprinting his way slowed for a moment; one even put his flaming sword back into its sheath. The angels gave each other bewildered looks, unsure exactly how to respond.

"Who are you? Are we supposed to know you?" one angel asked.

"I'm Malachi, Lucifer's new Chief of Staff."

"When did this happen?" asked one of the other approaching angels.

"Actually, it just did. I spirit leaped into this strategically important position so I could hopefully determine who controlled it. Glad to see it's already in your hands, and happy to see you're alert and prepared to fight to retain it. I'll make sure to include your names in my report when I deliver it to Lucifer."

Several of the angels began patting each other on the back. One said, "Sir, you need to be more careful now. Coming out here alone is definitely not a good idea anymore. You're lucky we didn't attack first and ask questions later."

"I can see that now. Clearly this wasn't my wisest move," answered Malachi.

One angel looked in the direction of the shrub to which Malachi had been crawling. He called out, "Hey Danyal, you just came from Adramelech's office, right?"

From his concealed position, a large angel with black wings stood to his feet. Though young in appearance, the angel still displayed the common emblems of an Archangel on his shoulder epaulettes. As the Archangel moved in his direction, Malachi got a queasy feeling in his stomach. *Oh no, I recognize this angel's face from the conference room.*

"It's you!" cried Danyal, drawing his flaming sword and rushing at Malachi. The other angels, shocked by their leader's reaction, at first remained motionless. Despite his fervor, the Archangel only covered a few yards before he suddenly stopped, let out an agonizing scream, and then disappeared in a burning cloud. When the smoke cleared, Corporal Joel stood where Danyal had been.

Several of Lucifer's followers turned towards Malachi with their weapons drawn. When they did, Malachi yelled, "What are you waiting for? Get him." The order confused the rebel angels enough to give Corporal Joel a chance to close the distance on two of them. Seconds later, flaming sword met flaming sword as Corporal Joel engaged one and then both of the rebels at once.

Four more of Lucifer's angels moved quickly into position to attack the corporal. The odds were overwhelming. Malachi had to take a chance, or they were certain to be defeated. To his left, Malachi noticed one particular enemy angel who was completely focused on his comrades and their combat with the corporal.

The angel screamed at Corporal Joel, "You fool. You should have run when you had the chance." The fallen angel's words turned obscene as he spurred his comrades on. With the fallen angel fully fixated on Corporal Joel's demise, Malachi spirit leaped into action, undetected by his target. Reappearing just behind the boisterous rebel, Malachi quickly withdrew the unsuspecting angel's sword from his sheath and thrust him through. There was no time for a scream, only an end to his ranting. He was simply gone, leaving his flaming sword in Malachi's hand.

Seeing their comrade dispatched by Malachi removed any doubt about the loyalties of their king's "new Chief of Staff." Three rebel angels moved quickly to exact a measure of revenge. As they broke formation and began circling their target, Malachi did the only thing he really knew to do: spirit leap to safety. His attempt proved futile and only drained what remained of his energy. He could manage only to fade from view for a moment, then reappear a few feet away. "Oh, trying to spirit leap away? You don't seem to be getting very far."

A second of the rebel angels added, "I think we need to take our time with this one. He didn't even give poor Ukobach enough respect to attack him face-to-face. Spirit leaped in behind him and stabbed him with his own sword."

"I agree. Let's destroy him slooowwwlyyyy…"

Malachi screamed, "You rebel against our King, and you speak of respect?"

"Your nammmee will beeee cuurrrssedd forrrreverrrrrrr," said the third angel as he circled Malachi.

"Stop with your taunts. If you mean to destroy me slowly, do it with your swords and not your words. I showed that much respect to your friend, whatever his name was." Before he finished his response, Malachi noticed something strange. It wasn't just that the angels who came against him were speaking slowly. Their bodies began to move in small jerking motions before they stopped altogether. When he ventured a glance at Corporal Joel, he and those he fought were like statues. Even the flock of gold-crested *ayit*, which soared overhead, appeared to be frozen in the sky even while they remained inexplicably aloft. All was silent and completely still.

"Do you know their names?" asked a calm and authoritative voice from behind Malachi, "The one you stabbed with his own flaming sword…his name is Ukobach. Right now he cries out in torment just beyond the eastern hills of the second heaven. And this one here is Xaphan. I know all of your names… because I created you."

Malachi spun around to see the source of the voice, but there was no one. Bewildered, he said, "There is only one Creator, our King, Elohim. Anyone who would claim otherwise is like these rebels."

"You speak wisely. Those who are Mine seek Me and find Me," came the voice once again from the opposite direction. "They have eyes which can still see and ears that can still hear. Can you still hear My voice? Can you still find Me, Malachi?"

The young angel was perplexed. "I can hear You, but where are You?" He began to spin in a circle, frantically seeking the One who called for him.

"I am, as always, close by you, Malachi. I have never left you nor will I ever leave you or forsake you."

It was then that he noticed something odd in the way the flaming swords of the soldiers who guarded him behaved. Only the flaming swords surrounding him flickered and waved to and fro, more like the ceremonial torches on the Holy Mount than the weapons of the rebels. Immediately, He fell to the ground in worship.

"Blessed are your eyes, because they see; and your ears, because they hear." The words came from all three flaming swords in perfect unison. Then, moving from one sword to the next in fast succession, the voices said:

"Blessed are the poor in spirit, for theirs is the kingdom of heaven."

"Blessed are those who hunger and thirst for righteousness, for they will be filled."

"Blessed are the pure in heart, for they will see God."

With his head still bowed, Malachi felt a gentle hand come to rest on his shoulder. He slowly looked up into a blinding light. A cloud swirled around the light, shielding Malachi from the blinding radiance of Yahweh. Malachi reached out his hand. As he did, the cloud thinned, revealing an outstretched hand. Malachi took hold of it and kissed it. He whispered, "Blessed beyond measure."

From out of the cloud stepped Yeshua, lifting Malachi to his feet as He appeared. The King said, "You still know and understand Me, Malachi...that I am the One who exercises loving kindness and righteousness in My kingdom. Lucifer's followers are now what I consider 'Fallen angels', and I can see in your heart that you are not one of them. Soon there will be even more revealed. But now, it is time for you to know and understand your true purpose. It is time for you to learn why I called you 'the One' on the day I created you."

Yeshua reached down and took the fallen angel's flaming sword from Malachi's hand, casting it into a nearby bush. As He did, the King said, "You have served Me well no matter where I have placed you, but those were roles I gave for just a moment." There suddenly appeared in Yeshua's grasp a sword with a blade that reached into the sky at a length nearly twice the size of those used by any other angel. With one hand on Malachi's shoulder, Yeshua placed the two-handed sword into Malachi hands. He gazed at his new weapon as the golden hilt reflected the King's radiance, a brilliance made even greater by the blood-red ruby affixed at its base. Yeshua touched the blade, and instantly, the sword was set ablaze with a bright golden flame.

No sooner had the sword's blade been kindled than did Yeshua disappear. Meanwhile, everything around Malachi came back to life, beginning with the three fallen angels who immediately continued their charge in his direction. In His mind, Malachi heard Yeshua's voice say, "Know your true identity…now. And begin to live it."

Three flaming swords suddenly plunged towards their target. Without a thought, Malachi blocked the blade of his first opponent, spun to escape the blow of the second angel, and then swung his own sword with all his might at the third. His long flaming sword shattered the blade of the third enemy before passing through the angel's body. The two remaining angels looked at one another with fear etched across their faces. Moments later, Malachi stood alone, his two foes having wisely chosen to retreat after witnessing the agonizing end of their defeated comrade.

Malachi looked at his sword. "How is it that I suddenly know how to fight?"

In his mind, the voice of Yeshua said, "When you get to the Archangel Michael's office, all will be revealed."

A short distance away, Corporal Joel prepared to take on the four fallen angels who opposed him. He bent to the ground and picked up a thick, broken tree branch, which split on one end to create a y-shaped tool of sorts. All four fallen angels attacked at once, the heat of their flaming swords sizzling as they cut through the air. Joel parried the initial thrust from his first opponent, catching his wrist in the forked end of the branch and pressing it to the ground. As he did so, he leaped into the air, kicking a second fallen angel in the chest and face, as he essentially ran across his enemy. The blows sent the fallen angel sprawling to the ground. Landing on his feet, Corporal Joel then blocked the thrust of a third attacker even as he twisted the tree branch he held in his offhand. The maneuver forced the flaming sword from the hand of the first attacker.

Corporal Joel turned to reposition himself for the next attack. As he did, the fourth fallen angel brought his sword down in what was certain to be a devastating blow. Inches before completing the strike, Malachi's flaming sword intervened, deflecting the blow away from Corporal Joel's head. In the same instant, Corporal Joel thrust his sword backwards into the fourth fallen angel, sending him into oblivion.

With three fallen angels facing the loyal servants of Elohim, the odds seemed to be evening out of bit. Yet, three more of Lucifer's warriors landed just in time to prevent Malachi from striking the first fallen angel whose flaming sword had been swept away by Corporal Joel.

"There are more of us to come," bragged one of the Fallen. "Can't you see how futile this struggle is for you? Stop now, and we might show some mercy. In fact, we might even give you a second chance to make a different choice regarding who you will serve."

"Our decision is made and is final," answered Corporal Joel.

The five fallen angels circled Malachi and Corporal Joel, while several others stood on the side planning their own attacks. One angel lifted his fiery sword high in the air, screaming, "For King Lucifer, and for Self." Suddenly an arrow crashed through the air, embedding itself in the fallen angel's raised hand. More arrows flew in from all directions, striking the five angels multiple times and sending the entire party off in a desperate flight back towards the Trade Room.

As they fled, twenty loyal angels landed beside Malachi and Corporal Joel. "We're sure glad to see you," said Malachi.

"Happy to help. We weren't sure which side you were on until Private Amos here recognized Corporal Joel. Follow us, and we'll take you to the Archangel Michael's office. I'm sure he will want to hear your story...and learn how you got your hands on these flaming weapons."

Malachi said, "I want to hear that one too, Corporal."

CHAPTER EIGHTEEN

WITHOUT EXCUSE

Once cleared by the sentries at the front doorway of the Archangel Michael's office, Malachi and Corporal Joel were escorted to a heavily guarded room. Two guardian angels stood at the front entrance while another four were stationed throughout the room. Between them sat the Archangel Michael, busily sending orders out to the field by way of messengers from the Archangel Gabriel's Department of Celestial Communications.

When the pace of Michael's efforts appeared to slow, the Corporal who brought Malachi and Joel to Michael's office stepped forward. "Sir, this is…"

"Hold that thought, Corporal. These orders must be synchronized perfectly or our entire line will collapse. In fact, right now is not the best time for introductions. We are about to start our command staff meeting. Have them come back later."

As he spoke, the room began to fill with Legion Commanders and Cohort Leads. From their appearance, covered in debris and showing signs of burnt clothing and skin, it was clear the fighting had been grueling.

Michael's aide leaned forward and whispered in his commander's ear.

For the first time, Michael's eyes left the map projecting up from his desk. Michael said, "They came from where? Wait. Stay. You might have something to add."

The Archangel began to update his officers on the most recent accounts from the front lines. "Initial reports present a bleak picture. Though our special forces have been well-trained, they are facing a desperate enemy. Not only that, but the fallen host appear to be armed with weapons which give them a significant advantage in combat. Some of you may have heard of their special flaming weapons. Our scouts have confirmed their existence and that they inflict considerably more damage than our iron weapons."

Corporal Joel raised his flaming sword in the air. "I have such a weapon."

"Where did you get one of those?" asked the officer to his right.

"I was wondering the same thing." Pulling his from its sheath, Malachi said, "I've had two. One I took off a rebel after I spirit leaped behind him for a surprise attack. He never expected the move. This one is a gift from Yeshua. Corporal, I have no idea how you got your flaming sword. I just know you showed up with one to save me during our escape. I thought you had been destroyed by Nergal. What happened?"

Corporal Joel looked at the Archangel for permission to speak. "Yes, Corporal. Please."

"When Nergal slashed at me with his flaming sword, I blocked the strike with my sword. Well actually, I was only able to partially deflect the blow. It was coming straight for my head when I decided I would be better served to spirit leap away."

Several of the officers suppressed a laugh as Corporal Joel continued, "I didn't care where I went at the time; just knew I needed to get out of there fast and to go to a place no one would expect."

The officer to Corporal Joel's left asked, "And, where was that?"

"I decided they would never search for me in Lucifer's favorite spot…the Garden of Eden. Fortunately, I was a little distracted when I began my leap and ended up a little off course. Instead of leaping among the fountains in Prayer Corner, I wound up on the backside of the garden. Interesting thing though. Where I reappeared was completely barren except for a huge, well, I guess you'd call it a lake. It didn't contain water. It was full of fire. I'm not sure how it got there."

"Interesting," said Malachi, "I did my mentorship on the backside of Eden… in an old, rundown cabin. Everything creaked, like it was falling apart. I came to realize things only made that awful sound when Lucifer was around. I wonder if that area finally broke down and became what Nergal called a lake of fire. He thought he was about to eliminate me as well. Guess he thought neither of us would ever be able to share their secret. Bragged that the lake was where they made their flaming weapons."

Corporal Joel added, "Trust me when I tell you. The lake is so hot, it's painful to approach. Still, I knew I needed a flaming sword like theirs if I was going to really be able to help you."

Michael ordered one of his soldiers, "Sergeant, dispatch one of the reserve cohorts with our remaining supply of swords and arrows. Once they've been dipped into the Lake of Fire, have them return as quickly as possible to distribute them to our forces."

"Yes, Sir."

"Thank you, angels." Michael returned to his briefing with his officers. "Many of our loyal angels have been driven to spirit leap just like Corporal Joel, without consideration for where they would end up. Sometimes their leaps placed them in the midst of rampaging hordes of rebels. Without any energy for another leap and completely surrounded, most of those angels were overtaken by the enemy. The brutality of the attacks against them is beyond description."

"Other reports from the front describe units loyal to our King encountering those of Lucifer. Many tried to talk the rebels down from their violent aims. In some cases, a few of the fallen angels acted as though they would surrender and return to the King's service. When this happened though, rebel leaders in the field directed attacks against them as well. It's as if the fallen angels have gone completely mad." Michael shook his head.

The Archangel waved his hand across his desk, calling up a three-dimensional map of heaven's six levels. "As the battles across the heavens have lingered, the front lines are swelling with new combatants for both sides in the conflict."

Malachi intently watched the map. Green and red lights seemed to race to strategic strongholds, communication hubs, and points used for traveling between the heavens. It seemed the number of dots for both colors was growing at an enormous rate. The green dots still clearly outnumbered the red, but the red dots were gaining more ground in every level, especially in the fourth heaven.

Malachi asked, "How did their numbers grow so large without me to aid them? No one I saw in Adramelech's conference room had the connections or know-how to raise an army that quickly."

Michael responded, "We've determined that several angels from the Department of Celestial Fellowship, and most of the angels who had won the King's Proclamation Award, were forced to provide the names and contact information of all angels who fit their targeted recruitment profile. Interestingly, several of Lucifer's followers who have been captured gave us the profiles they were seeking. Those they pursued most often were focused on advancement, undisciplined in their pursuit of time with the King, unwilling to stretch themselves by attempting projects that required complete dependence on Elohim, and those who struggled with discontentment."

As Malachi listened to the description, he thought to himself, *Those are traits I see in me. No wonder I considered joining the rebellion. But wait, did I? I did accept the Chief of Staff position offered by Lucifer, and I did follow him out of the Assembly Chamber when Yeshua condemned his ideas and actions.* Malachi shook his head to chase the thoughts from his mind.

As he continued to watch the movement of forces on Michael's map, Malachi began to see a pattern form. He asked the Archangel, "How long are you going to delay Lucifer from getting to the Holy Mount, and how long until you release his fallen angels so they can head our way?"

"Very observant," said Michael. "It's Malachi, right? You mentioned escaping from Adramelech's offices. Tell me what you know."

"Lucifer took me to the back conference room of his office. I saw thirty or more angels gathered around the conference table." He then named those he recognized while several of Michael's aides took notes.

Michael nodded. "That gives us a good idea of who else may have followed Lucifer. He's actually been planning this for a while; just looking for the right excuse to turn on the King. Seems Lucifer took the King's bait."

Malachi and Corporal Joel looked at each other in astonishment. Michael explained, "Elohim knew long ago that Lucifer wanted to stop worshipping Him. Instead, he's been worshipping himself while convincing others to do the same. As it turns out, the King has been waiting for just the right level of frustration to rise in Lucifer's arrogant and prideful heart; waiting for him to act upon his deepest desire. He doesn't want to be the greatest angel. He doesn't even want to be treated like a god. He wants to replace God. That means overthrowing Elohim. The creation of man was just the tipping point that forced Lucifer to reveal this deepest intention of his heart. It also allowed any other angels who harbored similar sentiments to reveal themselves.

"Malachi, Elohim knew Lucifer would approach angels who were well connected across numerous departments. There was no way to allow Lucifer and those angels who would fall for his bribes and deceptions to follow through except to let some of you go through your interview process. The King specifically put you in their minds as their top choice because you fit their profile, but also because He knew you would be able to stand up against the temptation. He knew it would be close; that you would likely need some support from another angel to pull it off, but Elohim knew your heart was devoted to Him. That's the reason why He called you 'the One' when He created you. You would be the one who could stand up to the temptation and later be able to tell of everything that transpired throughout this entire rebellion."

Malachi couldn't believe what he was hearing. "If He's known of Lucifer's intentions for a while, why did Elohim wait so long to bring things to a head? And, why not just end the rebellion immediately?"

"Well, Malachi, for one, Elohim wants to make sure Lucifer has no excuse for the judgment he will face in the future. Our King will win this war. It's important that Lucifer is not able to somehow say he wouldn't follow through on his evil intentions. Unfortunately, he did follow through, and now we are at war. There are some who, like you, were on the fence. Elohim knows who will turn to Lucifer and who will remain loyal to Him. The decision to be loyal is individual and personal. Elohim wants every angel who would choose to follow Him to do so without coercion. He is determined that we will never have a doubt about whom they would choose to serve. I'll ask you to do what He asked of me; trust Him and know that His timing is always perfect."

Malachi thought about the circumstances that had led to him standing in front of Michael. He never wanted to stop following Elohim, but the allure of Self and other ideas presented by Lucifer was so strong. He looked at Corporal Joel and said, "I'm sure glad Elohim didn't cut your entry into that conference room any closer. I was at war within myself."

"I know your heart now. You never would have walked away from Elohim." Joel patted Malachi on the back as he ushered his new friend closer to the image of the heavens which rose above Michael's desk. Joel asked, "So what did you see that made you ask Michael about Lucifer's arrival at the Holy Mount and the fallen coming here?"

"I noticed the units that were listed as trained in the last six months were giving ground faster than the other units in the field. It was subtle, but it stood to reason that perhaps this was by design. It looks like a weakness in our line was allowing Lucifer to go to the place he would naturally want to go. If those troops were specifically trained for this type of a situation, I find it hard to believe they would be the weak points."

"Good deduction, Malachi," said Michael. "That is exactly the King's strategy. He knows Lucifer wants to attack us at the Holy Mount and here at my offices. What Lucifer doesn't realize is that his plan wasn't hatched in the minds of Moloch and Semiazas of their own accord. Elohim is sovereign, even in a situation such as this. Those units which were specially trained for this situation know they are to lure Lucifer to the place He wants to go. Lucifer wants it, but only because Elohim wants it as well. Now, we will see if it was the right plan based on how easily we can subdue the rebels at both locations. Obviously, we are confident. The King is on our side. With Him, all things are possible."

CHAPTER NINETEEN

THE FIRST VOLLEY

"And there was war in heaven, Michael and his angels
waging war with the dragon..."

Revelation 12:7a

Tensions ran high as the lead units along the pathways from the Trade Room to both the Holy Mount and Michael's offices gave ground right up to their final defensive positions.

Fighting was intense up and down the entire front, but these two locations were now the focal points of the conflict. As angelic units from the Army of the Host fell back slowly along these two pathways, Lucifer's Fallen angels rushed in to take advantage of what looked to be an obvious weakness.

Watching from the Holy Mount, Elohim thought, *Lucifer believes he has the upperhand. Soon he will know the truth. Let the wise one boast not of his wisdom, nor the strong one boast of his strength, nor the rich one boast of his riches, but let he who boasts, boast of this...that he knows and understands Me. Oh Lucifer, you do not know Me.*

As the rebellion gained momentum, the delineation between angels in support of the King and those who threw their lot in with Lucifer became increasingly clear. Angels began to declare their loyalties at a rapid pace, either defending the King or trying to bring Him down. Finally, as this long, Lost Day, reached its eleventh hour, Elohim summoned a Heralding Angel and delivered a simple statement to be shared with every loyal angel throughout the heavens. Calmly, the Heralding Angel passed the message on to the many messenger angels that stood by outside the Holy Mount, waiting for their turn to deliver a message to the front from the King. One-by-one, the messenger angels lifted into the sky or spirit leapt to their assigned units. When they arrived, they simply read:

The hour has come.
All have declared.
Let loose the Lion.

With that message, Elohim signaled that every angel in the heavens had aligned either with Him or with Lucifer.

Upon receiving the message, Michael cried out in a loud voice, "The Lion has roared, who will not fear?" The message spread down the line of angels as each passed it along to his comrade. All knew what it meant. The time had come to spring their trap. One at a time, and then in pairs, angels began to leave the defensive line in front of Michael's office, falling back to a prepared position within the offices. Meanwhile, several cohorts fell back out of the offices into a prepared position behind the building. To any who may have been watching, it looked as if the defending force walked through Michael's office and retreated even further to the rear. In reality, the warriors of the King were ideally positioned to defend the office, and then counterattack once the enemy's position became tenuous.

Spirits were high along the defensive front of the Army of the Host. Still, all were silent as Michael's forces waited in anticipation of combat. Each angel looked to his right and left for encouragement. A similar scene took place on the Holy Mount, but in that setting, each angel looked not to his comrades, but to the King.

******

Suddenly, the air was filled with fire as if the heavens themselves were set ablaze. Streaking through the sky were flaming arrows numbering more than the sands of the seashore; however, they weren't being launched by the Army of the Host. Instead, it was the opening salvo by Lucifer's army in their attack on Michael's offices. Though many of the arrows fell harmlessly against the defensive walls, many found their marks. Screams of pain filled the air as thousands of angels felt the scorching heat of the Lake of Fire.

Malachi cringed as the memory of his own encounter with a flaming sword intruded into his mind.

Corporal Joel grabbed Malachi's arm and said, "I'll do all I can to keep you from experiencing that again. Still, this is an hour for sacrifice. I know you are willing to give everything for our King. I question if our enemies have as much resolve for Lucifer."

Malachi nodded in agreement. Thinking of how close he came to joining the rebellion alongside Lucifer, he responded, "Don't worry about me. I will give everything I am to uphold the throne of Elohim."

Together, Malachi and Corporal Joel walked along the defensive front, providing aid to all the suffering even as they dodged incoming arrows. As they did, Malachi heard several angels raising an alarming concern:

"How is it that Lucifer's army knew just when and where to strike us?"

"I thought our plan set a trap for them. It feels like it was a trap for us."

"Did the enemy know our plan? It seemed like the timing of their attack couldn't have been any better."

Malachi led Corporal Joel aside and said, "I have to admit, it did seem strange how the initial volley came just after we received our new orders."

"We should make sure the Archangel knows about these rumors. We may have a traitor in our ranks."

They made their way back to the makeshift command center in the office of Archangel Michael's deputy assistant. It had been decided that using his own office would not be wise, given how readily the enemy would know of its location. As the two approached the office, they were met by five guardian angels in full battle armor.

"Halt, identify yourself!" came the forceful order from the angel who was obviously in command of the security detail.

"Malachi and Corporal Joel."

"They are the new ones, Sir," said one of the other warriors in the security detail.

"Stay right where you are," ordered the commander.

"Why the harsh treatment, Commander?" asked Corporal Joel.

"Well Corporal, you might have noticed there are a lot of angels who aren't quite who they seem anymore. And this one you are with…well, he just happens to be the angel Lucifer named to be his Chief of Staff."

"I understand why you are being so cautious, but I believe he's proven his loyalty to the King by now," replied Corporal Joel.

The commander of the detail then said, "I tell you what. Let's go visit the Archangel Michael together and clear up this matter. You lead the way."

Slowly, the two loyal servants of Elohim, who had already suffered so much in defense of the throne, suffered the indignity of being taken under armed watch to the hallway leading to the office of the deputy assistant. As Malachi reached for the door handle, one of the warriors asked, "Why have you led us here? This isn't the office of the Archangel. It's not on this hallway."

Malachi slowly turned to face the five warriors, a determined look on his face. "What are you doing, Malachi?" asked Corporal Joel.

"Don't you think the security detail for the Archangel would know where he was? Yet, these traitors want us to take them to the Archangel's office." Turning to the angels of the security detail, he asked, "And, where were you when I was taking the first stand against this rebellion?"

"I shouldn't answer you, but I will. We were at our stations, carrying out our orders. Much more than what you've been doing…traitor."

"I'm sure you were, but whose orders were you carrying out, Asmodeus?" asked Malachi as he drew his flaming sword and thrust at the angel who stood before them. Asmodeus dodged the strike and drew his own sword.

Corporal Joel asked, "Who are these angels?"

"Traitors. They serve Lucifer now." Before he could say more, the warriors of the security detail drew their swords and moved to engage Malachi. Drawing his own sword, Corporal Joel jumped once more to Malachi's side.

"I don't know who these two angels are," said Malachi, pointing at the angels on their flanks, "but these three are Asmodeus, Sammael, and Ahriman. They were in the Trade Room when you rescued me."

Sammael immediately stuttered, "Uh…you must be…I was never…"

Ahriman, shaking his head, placed a hand on his comrade and said, "Sammael, we knew it would eventually come to this. Let's get started."

Asmodeus stepped in front of Sammael and Ahriman, and said, "Perceptive. With all those angels present and us in the background, how could you have recognized us?"

"I may be just a low-ranking angel, but I am a low-ranking associate in the Department of Celestial Fellowship. Recognizing those attending a function at which I am in attendance is…well, my job."

Asmodeus said, "Well, my job is to drive the Archangel from this position and to do the same with any angels who might get in our way. So, what will it be? Take an unwise stand against a bigger force or flee without having to feel the flames of my sword?"

"Guess I'll have to take yet another stand," said Malachi. "I will never bow to Lucifer or cower before the advances of you who try to disgrace Elohim."

"That's just what your boss said before we ran him through and led him away. Don't worry, I'm sure you both will see Barnabas soon."

While Asmodeus, Sammael, and Ahriman feinted attacks at Malachi and Corporal Joel, the fallen angels on their flanks rushed forward, attempting to catch the two by surprise. Instead, they met the flaming swords of two angels who had already experienced combat. Corporal Joel dispatched the fallen angel, attacking him with a devastating blow to the head before the enemy could even begin to strike. Malachi blocked his attacker's blow, producing glowing embers. As he prepared to finish the fight with his own attack, the fallen warrior spirit leaped away.

Before the sparks settled, Sammael and Ahriman pressed forward in a lightning-fast strike which caught Malachi and Corporal Joel by surprise. While Sammael swung his flaming sword at Malachi's head, Ahriman slid along the ground swinging at Corporal Joel's legs. Both strikes glanced off their targets, causing the two servants of Elohim to step back in pain. Fortunately, the strikes didn't leave them incapacitated.

While Elohim's angels tried to regain their bearings, Asmodeus flew forward with a strike of his own. Just as the sword was about to find its mark across Malachi's back, Corporal Joel extended his own sword to foil the blow at the last second. He then spun out of his defensive maneuver into an attack on Sammael. Though his attack on Malachi had been fast enough to sneak past his defenses, Sammael's strike met its match in the speed of Corporal Joel's counter. Moments later, there remained only Asmodeus and Ahriman.

As the four remaining combatants faced off, from out of nowhere, the fallen angel chased initially from the fight by Malachi now reappeared behind him. In an instant, all three struck out at the two angels. Only the skill of Corporal Joel prevented an immediate victory by the opponents. As he battled on the ground against Asmodeus and Ahriman, Malachi reengaged his battle with the recently returned Fallen angel in a mid-air duel.

Malachi's opponent attempted to spirit leap behind him again; however, Malachi anticipated the maneuver and thrust his flaming sword in a reverse strike. The fallen angel reappeared at just the right moment and location to find himself impaled on Malachi's flaming sword. The defeated warrior lingered in his agonizing state even after Malachi pulled his sword free from his body.

Meanwhile, Corporal Joel, despite his great skill, could do little more than fend off Asmodeus and Ahriman. Finding himself cornered and unable to gain the upper hand with his blade, he must have remembered Malachi's actions during his fight with Nergal. Still wielding his sword, the corporal began to speak blessings upon the fallen angels.

Instantly, the unsuspecting followers of Lucifer fell to their knees, begging for mercy. Unfortunately for them, Corporal Joel's flaming blade was swifter than their cries. Both were sliced through, disappearing in a burst of fire.

"They were surrendering," said Malachi, "couldn't you have spared them those final blows?"

"I would have been happy to do so," responded the corporal. "Guess they need to surrender faster next time."

Alone in the hallway in front of the office of Michael's deputy assistant, the two angels knocked and then entered the makeshift command center.

"What was that racket in the hallway?" asked the Archangel.

Malachi answered, "Sir, we were coming to warn you that a traitor among us has been informing the enemy of our plans. We believe this information allowed them to effectively time their initial volley against our positions."

"Do you have any idea who might be serving Lucifer within my command?"

"I do, but I'm almost certain they won't be troubling you again." Malachi and Corporal Joel explained their encounter with Michael's security detail and their planned strike against his position.

"I'll be needing some replacements to guard me during this battle. Know anyone I can trust?" asked the Archangel Michael. "Never mind. The two of you will be perfect."

CHAPTER TWENTY

FRONTAL ASSAULT

"The dragon and his angels waged war..."
Revelation 12:7b

For those whose lives are lived with an eternal perspective, the concept of a day is pointless. Yet, this Lost Day, which began with the devastation of the first volley loosed on Michael's defenses at the direction of spies in the Archangel's ranks, not only stood out, but seemed to linger endlessly. Those not injured by the fiery arrows of that first strike or the endless waves which followed did what they could to aid their suffering comrades. Teams of angels entered disputed space between the opposing lines, sometimes even under the terms of a momentary ceasefire, in hopes of aiding the injured. Despite these agreements, the rescue teams found themselves under attack, even when helping members of Lucifer's forces. It was obvious no aid could be provided until victory was won, and unfortunately, victory appeared fleeting everywhere along Elohim's defensive line.

As the spirits of the Army of the Host began to sink with the lingering cries of comrades left alone in disputed space, a chilling sound began to rise from the ranks of the fallen angels. So eerie was the cackle of their laughter that some angels fled without ever being struck, morale being almost completely destroyed. Frontline commanders for the Army of the Host began to see huge gaps open all along their defensive perimeter.

Finally, when it seemed like the vast majority of Michael's defensive force was incapacitated by injury or fear, Lucifer's warriors crashed through and into what remained of his core defense. Some flew in at top speed while others spirit leaped into the faces of the building's defenders.

The first wave of this new, frontal assault on Michael's office caught many off guard. A large number of defenders believed the enemy would need time to mount another significant attack. As a result, they were busy looking for lost comrades following the earlier arrow barrages they had endured. Those who were focused on defending their positions were overcome by the sheer speed of the attack. Screams filled the air as the King's host felt the sting of yet another dramatic blow to their numbers.

Even the bravest of angels began to retreat deeper into the building, looking for cover from the rainstorm of arrows and the strikes coming from the swords of their winged pursuers. Some just looked for a clear avenue of escape. As a second defensive perimeter was being set, a new fresh line of the fallen angels stepped past their comrades from the first assault.

While the first wave of attackers had been large, this new line of fallen angels threatened to drown out the glory of Elohim on the battlefield. Many of the injured who lay in the field of battle fell silent out of fear. Standing in front of their bewildered opponent, dressed in dull-red body armor, the members of this special unit of the fallen angels, known as "Our Thundering Voice," all spoke a curse against Michael's defense front. Again, they tore huge holes in what remained of the Army of the Hosts' lines. Those who remained reeled backwards under the force of the oppression that filled the air. Many others writhed on the ground, unable to gather their wits as the pain of unholy power coursed through their spirits.

******

Malachi and Corporal Joel watched from their position guarding Michael's command center as some angels pressed on despite the torment of their injuries. Still others, even sometimes the strongest and bravest, could not take the agony and spirit leaped away from the fray.

Despite his own resolve, Malachi thought, *I can't blame them for fleeing. Any who would question their faithful service has not felt the flaming sword, flaming arrow, or this power of blessings and curses. Only those who have suffered understand the immense sacrifice they have given for our King.*

For all practical purposes, the defenses at Michael's offices had broken, and this dreadful, this Lost Day, appeared to be truly...lost.

******

Lucifer, leading the primary force of fallen angels towards the Holy Mount, bypassed the Mount of the Assembly. As per the plan that he, Moloch, and

Semiazas had devised, he would return to take it once Yahweh had capitulated. The defenses leading to the Holy Mount seemed far less organized and were surprisingly putting up less resistance. He and many of the Watchers forced their way through the sixth heaven.

Lucifer shouted to his followers, "Well done, warriors! We've taken the King completely by surprise. We've already stormed through the higher heavens, and word has come that our second command has cornered Michael and driven off many of the defenders at his position. We're prepared to take the Holy Mount. It's just a matter of time now. Soon, I will be your king, and you will finally receive the benefits of *Self.*"

Lucifer and his closest followers approached the gate to the Holy Mount. Rage filled his heart, and he yelled, "For all you have taken from me, I will pour down my wrath." Rather than opening the gate, he sliced through it with his flaming sword.

As he did, Nergal arrived on the scene. Though battered, Nergal was proving to be one of the best at infiltrating enemy territory and gathering intelligence. He reported, "Sir, the enemies defending the Archangel Michael have broken. We are victorious in the Administrative District of the fourth heaven. All that remains for us to take is the Mount of the Assembly. However, there are so few defenders left, it should fall without much effort. The first, second, and third heavens are in complete disarray. We have close to one-third of all angels now following our cause. The leadership structure of those who remain loyal to the King has been thrown into chaos. Entire angelic departments have shut down, and fear runs rampant among our enemies. They simply don't know who to trust anymore. Our efforts are working perfectly. All we need to do now is to force the King to surrender."

His report bolstered Lucifer's confidence, and he cried out in a loud voice, "I will make myself like the Most High God!"

Nergal said, "If I may be so bold, may I be the first to say, 'Hail, King Lucifer.'"

******

As the forces under Lucifer drove themselves toward the temple, several waves of the fallen angels easily broke through the Guardian Cherubim who fought to secure the steps leading up the Holy Mount. Lucifer raised his flaming sword and urged his command to launch themselves up the climb and on to their ultimate prize: Yahweh Himself. Lucifer was certain he would be in His rightful seat on the throne in no time at all.

Angels trained especially for just this moment soared into action to prevent the unrighteous from defiling the Holy Mount; however, the force of Lucifer's desires, as well as the words of his cursing, easily drove even these elite angels from the field. With none to hinder his progress up the steps towards the temple, Lucifer once more basked in the glory that he was certain would be his. Far above the glory which would come to the ruler over all the angels, Lucifer raised his sword in imminent victory and cried out, "No longer will I serve another. In fact, Yahweh will serve me."

******

The battle still raged within the offices of the Archangel Michael, as the King's host began to break into independent bands of unorganized resistance. Several of these small bands of angels put up heroic efforts for their King and for their brothers-in-arms; however, they quickly learned that evil intentions allow a level of ruthlessness in combat that is hard to match. That is, until ruthlessness meets righteous indignation.

CHAPTER TWENTY-ONE

COUNTERATTACK

"and they were not strong enough…"
Revelation 12:8a

Inside the marble hallway at his offices, the Archangel Michael stepped through the chaotic crowd of mostly retreating members of the Army of the Host. Driven by what Malachi was certain must be loyalty to Elohim, the Archangel walked straight through several blows delivered by the enemies of the King. Malachi was amazed that, despite the obvious pain, Michael kept his eyes fixed on the forces of evil that now threatened His Creator. It was clear the Archangel's intentions were to prevent the Host of God from breaking, even if he had to do it alone.

Michael cut through the horde of fallen angels with his flaming sword like light cuts through the darkness. Unable to stand alone against him, an organized group of fallen angels, two hundred swords strong, spirit leaped onto and all around the determined warrior. Michael fought with all that was within him, but these odds were even more than he could stand.

When all seemed lost, two angels threw themselves into the flash and fury that surrounded Michael. Malachi and Corporal Joel took up positions beside and to the rear of Michael, creating a fortress of sorts against their attackers. Michael regained his footing, and the three angels began to push back the rebels and thwart their progress against the Army of the Host.

Flaming swords, flaming arrows, and the use of the Power of Blessings and Curses, the name that the angels gave to the vocalized weapon which Ruach Elohim first taught to Malachi, slowly gave way to massive hand-to-hand combat. The spirit beings on both sides broke into one-on-one battles where neither would succumb, despite the agony inflicted on each other. Finally, a reorganized defense formed around Michael, Malachi, and Joel, pushing the fallen angels from the building and back into the disputed space of the courtyard. The exhausted forces eyed one another and readied to battle once again.

All at once, there was a thunderous sound and a blast of holy light.

******

The Holy Mount of God came ablaze with fire and light. With a power that blew everyone back and halted all fighting, the King commanded, "Kneel!"

Every angel on the Holy Mount fell to the ground, compelled there by an unseen force. But this was not low enough for Yahweh. Soon, by the sheer power of His will, every angel from both sides of the conflict felt compelled to lie completely prostrate on their faces. Even Lucifer, with all his power and pride, was unable to fight the compulsion to fall on his face before the One who was, is, and always would be the sovereign Lord and King of all.

For all his misplaced pride and deluded visions of grandeur, Lucifer remained completely dependent upon his Creator. He had ascended to the base of the Holy Mount in the strength of his deeply held, but erroneous, belief in his superiority to Elohim.

More so, he actually believed he could stand against His omnipotent King, his elevated sense of Self allowing him to rationalize his actions and justify his treason. Despite these misconceptions, when he came face-to-face with the One who had bestowed upon him all manner of blessing, Lucifer's power was like a leaf being swept in a downward plunge over the edge of a waterfall.

Yahweh revealed the fullness of His glory. As He did, He peered down at Lucifer and his followers who were lying before Him on the ground and declared, "To which of My angels have I ever said, 'Sit at My right hand or My left hand, until I make Your enemies a footstool for Your feet?'"

To these words, the Heralding Angel added, "Let all the angels of God worship Him."

These words officially ended the rebellion of the Lost Day.

CHAPTER TWENTY-TWO

THE TRIAL

"...and there was no longer a place found for them in heaven."
Revelation 12:8b

T he rattle of chains, the shuffle of feet, and the slamming of the gavel. Such were the sounds associated with hundreds of fallen angels going to trial. Guards led the long procession of angels who rebelled against the King one-by-one to the Assembly Chamber. There they were called to stand before their Judge, Yeshua, and make a defense for their actions on the Lost Day. Though their only hope lay in the grace and mercy of their King, none repented of their actions. With hardened hearts, the prisoners saw no need to seek forgiveness, regardless of the potential punishment.

Each was formally charged with treason, tried and convicted, and then sentenced to a punishment to be named upon completion of all other trials associated with the rebellion. The ultimate sentence was to remain unannounced until the last of the fallen angels, Lucifer, was brought before the throne of His King and Judge.

While every angel overflowed with nervous anticipation, none felt it more so than Malachi and Corporal Joel. It had been their charge to serve as key witnesses for the King at the trials of each and every member of the Fallen, as the members of the rebellion had come to be known. As the only two eyewitnesses to the events in the Trade Room, in addition to their being significant combatants on the Lost Day, it was Malachi's and Corporal Joel's testimonies which sealed the eternal destiny of many of the Watchers and other members of the Fallen. And now, that responsibility meant testifying against the Angel of Light.

Malachi met Corporal Joel on the steps leading up to the front doorway of the Assembly Chamber. "One last time, my friend."

"True. I thought it would never end."

"How long has it been, Joel?"

"I stopped keeping track after the first one thousand cases." The corporal half-grinned and shook his head.

"As much as I want this to end, I've been dreading this day."

"I know, Malachi, and I understand why."

"I just know Lucifer is going to attack me because of my acceptance of his Chief of Staff position. He will say I should be on trial as well. For all I know, he's right."

Corporal Joel earnestly shook his head. "We've been through all this before. You made your choice when you stood against Lucifer both at the Trade Room and in the battles which followed. None can say you didn't remain loyal to the King in the end. Remember what Michael said on the Lost Day. You were chosen by the King to be 'the One' who would walk beside Lucifer throughout his descent from Angel of Light to the first of the Fallen. You were 'the One' who would witness it all, see the full depth of his depravity, and yet stand against him…despite the bribes offered your way. Elohim placed you in that position because He knew you would ultimately remain loyal to Him."

"I know what He said about me. I just can't believe I was so foolish as to even consider joining with Lucifer and his unrighteous hordes." Malachi shook his head in shame as they entered the Assembly Chamber. As they took their seats in the gallery section reserved for witnesses, Malachi whispered, "I still know this will be a very uncomfortable day."

Corporal Joel replied, "Don't worry. I'm here with you. More importantly, Ruach Elohim will be with you throughout the proceedings."

******

Lucifer was led into the Assembly Chamber, his wrists bound in chains. The sight of the Angel of Light in such a state was difficult for many angels to comprehend. This was the one from among them who actually walked side-by-side with Yahweh among the fiery stones on the Holy Mount, and the one who for millennia led the worship of Elohim.

Every celestial being was completely thrown off balance not knowing what was to come. After an existence of complete peace and contentment, suddenly, in a single moment, the leadership structure of the angelic hierarchy was thrust into total chaos. Prior to these trials, throughout all of eternity past, the heavens and every created being had only experienced the loving kindness and holiness of Elohim. Now, for the first time, they were seeing other aspects of His nature. Perfect in justice. Impartial in His judgments. Even those who did not rebel against Him were shaken by the sight of Elohim filled with righteous indignation.

Despite the unsettling effects of seeing the perfect justice of Elohim on display, every loyal angel wanted to be present at Lucifer's trial. Still, Elohim saw fit to allow only a very specific group of angels to attend the proceedings. Angels who played a significant part in the combat of the Lost Day or eyewitnesses to acts of significant brutality were given first priority. Malachi and Joel were invited based on this criteria.

Others were invited because they belonged to one of the three classes of angels which most often participated in the rebellion. This list included primarily angels who were Cherubim, Powers (or Authorities), or Principalities (or Rulers). Interestingly, in interviews with those who rebelled from among the Powers and Principalities, it was found that "selfish ambition" was most often cited as their reason. Powers, being in the lowest third of the second sphere saw little chance of ever receiving a promotion to the highest sphere. Likewise, Principalities, though being the highest angels in the third sphere, saw promotion as just a step into the lowest class of the second sphere, from which an upward move would likely never end in promotion to the third sphere.

The King's intent was purposeful. The fallen angels were now imperfect, unredeemable, and therefore now and forever, no longer compatible with Him as a perfect God. Elohim wanted the angels of these classes who remained loyal to see for themselves the character of the one who led their brethren into their lost state, and the extent to which the King actually went in trying to preserve them all from their miserable destiny.

When all were present who were needed for this unprecedented moment in pre-time history, the Heralding Angel stepped into the room and called, "All rise. To Elohim, our Creator, Sustainer, and still Sovereign King be all glory, both now and forever."

Though Lucifer and the Fallen tried to hiss and curse at the announced entry of the King, none were able to do so. An indescribable power kept them humbly mute. Throughout the Assembly Chamber, a reverent hush fell over all who waited with anticipation for the entrance of Elohim.

Suddenly the Godhead Trinity appeared on the elevated terrace, a position which once more reminded all that there was a clear difference between the

Creator and His creation. It was something that needed to be reiterated in light of the events of the Lost Day. It was a concept that had clearly escaped Lucifer. For such forgetfulness and the subsequent hardening of his heart towards Elohim, Lucifer would pay a high price.

During all of the previous trials involving each of the fallen angels, Yeshua simply listened and passed judgment while seated on His throne. But now, with Lucifer at the stand, the King remained on His feet. It was an ominous sight which made several angels remark after the proceedings at just how "terrifying it must be to fall into the hands of the Living God." Lucifer was now the target of Elohim's righteous anger, and he would experience what that was like firsthand.

The Heralding Angel stood before the court. "Our Creator, King, and now Judge, before you stands one who has been blameless in all his ways from the day he was created until unrighteousness permeated his heart, leading him to orchestrate the events of what we now call the Lost Day. He is charged with treason. Lucifer, how do you plead?"

In a harsh voice which betrayed the state of his heart, Lucifer responded, "Not guilty, and everyone knows it."

At this, Yeshua said, "The defendant will please hold his remarks to just those necessary to answer the questions he is asked. No commentary please."

Yeshua said to Lucifer, "You had the seal of perfection, full of wisdom and perfect in beauty. You were in Eden, My Garden. Every precious stone was your covering—the ruby, the topaz, and the diamond, the beryl, the onyx, and the jasper; the lapis lazuli, the turquoise, and the emerald; and the gold, the workmanship of your settings, and sockets—all were in you. On the day you were created they were prepared."

Once more Lucifer sat in the presence of Elohim as all of the glory of His King was revealed. It was blinding, even brighter than his experience of it just days before when the King announced His intention to create man. In reality, the King was constantly veiling His true glory. If He did not do so, regardless of the realm, His radiance would destroy His creations.

Even in the face of unmatched splendor and holiness, Lucifer remained wrapped up in himself. His heart hardened even more because of the devastating effects of the arrogance and pride that lay within him. It corrupted him to the core. He still looked at himself and perceived the glory of God revealed in that moment as originating from…himself.

The King looked at Lucifer, the angel He had promoted to the Holy Mount and whom He had assigned the privilege of leading the worship presented to Him for such a long time. The King looked beyond the surface. He looked into his heart to the depth of his motives. It was all too clear.

Elohim knew the condition of Lucifer's heart, of every heart within each member of the Fallen. There would be no pardon. There could be no pardon. So strong was Lucifer's influence and control over those who had succumbed to his alluring ideas regarding the preeminence of Self that none of them could ever be reconciled with God. They would always fight Him. They were unredeemable.

******

Yeshua, acting as both the Judge and the Prosecutor, began His case against Lucifer. By this point, the evidence and testimony against Lucifer was beyond refutation, especially after Corporal Joel's eyewitness testimony of what transpired in the Trade Room. Despite the open-and-shut nature of the case, Yeshua pressed further than what seemed necessary, having Malachi called to the stand.

Nervous energy rushed throughout the Assembly Chamber. By now, all knew of the young angel's acceptance of the Chief of Staff position serving Lucifer on the Lost Day. Many questioned why he too had not been placed on trial. Most assumed the King offered him mercy in exchange for his testimony. Even Malachi wondered, *Why is the King placing me on the stand? He's subjecting me to what is certain to be accusations by the Fallen—by Lucifer himself.*

Still, Malachi made his way to the witness stand as he had for every other member of the Fallen.

Yeshua began, "Please describe for those in attendance the nature of your relationship to the defendant."

"Well, my relationship to Lucifer is different from any I have with other defendants in these trials. While some were friends, most were relationships forged out of my work at the Department of Celestial Fellowship."

Yeshua continued, "What was different about your relationship with Lucifer?"

Malachi nervously cleared his throat, then answered, "Lucifer was my transitional mentor ages ago when it came time for me to move from a local support angel to my kingdom support status. During that time, I met with Lucifer daily..."

Yeshua interrupted, "And, where was it that you met Lucifer?"

Malachi explained their rendezvous in the rundown cabin in the Garden of

Eden. "I believe it was on the very spot where the Lake of Fire is today."

Yeshua nodded. "Didn't you find such a meeting place odd?"

Malachi was beginning to wonder if Yeshua was about to reverse things and place him on trial with the rest of the defendants. Amid his hesitation in answering the question, Yeshua repeated His query.

"Yes, I did wonder about it. In the beginning, it seemed odd, but then it seemed like a good way to keep our relationship private; easier to meet without angels always making a big deal of our relationship. Towards the end though, when word was pretty much out, I did wonder why we didn't meet in the main offices of the Garden of Eden. I still wonder."

"Wasn't it during those meetings with Lucifer that you first were introduced to his concept of Self?"

Malachi was confused. *Where is Yeshua going with this questioning? Should I have done something differently back then? Should I have immediately told someone that Lucifer had these thoughts?* Cautiously, Malachi answered, "Yes, that is where he first raised the idea to me. It's also where he first expressed a desire to make his will of greater importance than Your own."

"Did you feel Lucifer was inappropriate at that time?"

"I did, and I started to walk out over it. However, he convinced me that perhaps failing to do my will when it was in conflict with Your will would actually introduce imperfection into Your kingdom. I thought perhaps he was correct when he said You preferred us to choose our will over Your will at times in order to maintain perfection in the kingdom. I know now that was just Lucifer manipulating me; however, at the time, to an inexperienced angel such as myself, it did seem logical on some level."

"What of the meeting you attended in what is now being referred to as the 'Trade Room'? Was Lucifer there, and what did he say?"

Malachi shared of all he had witnessed, from the admission on Lucifer's part that he was pursuing his will over the King's to the call to rise up and fight for self-rule. As testimony goes, it was quite damning to Lucifer and his case. So effective was Malachi's testimony that when he finished, Yeshua rested His case. Now, all waited to see how Lucifer would counter the testimony.

CHAPTER TWENTY-THREE

REBUTTAL

"...When he lies, he speaks out of his own character,
for he is a liar and the father of lies."

John 8:44b

T
he Angel of Light stood and approached the witness stand. As he did, the hair on Malachi's neck stood on end. His heart beat faster and sweat began to form on his forehead. Now eye-to-eye with his former mentor and friend, Malachi awaited the attack he knew was to come. *The only question that remains is how will Yeshua respond?*

Lucifer began, "Malachi, we've known each other a long time, right?"

"Yes."

"On what occasion did we first meet?"

"As I shared with Yeshua, it happened at the time of my transitional mentorship."

"What ideas did I share with you at that time?"

"Well, there were quite a few ideas we discussed."

"I think you know which ideas I am referring to. Do you remember us speaking about Self? Do you recall the reason I shared for why doing our own will is an important part of maintaining the perfection of heaven?"

"Yes, I do."

"So then, is it true that, on the basis of your agreement with those ideas, you accepted my Chief of Staff position? Remember, Malachi...you're before Elohim. All is laid bare. There is only truth."

Malachi thought about Lucifer's question. There was really only one way to answer while still speaking the whole truth. "Yes, I did accept the Chief of Staff position. You were quite influential in the way you presented the concepts. I believed I was helping meet Elohim's ultimate purposes better by pursuing my will above His own...at least some of the time."

"Do you really expect this court to believe you when you make such a statement? You really believed you were doing His will by denying it to pursue your own?"

"As I said, you were quite persuasive."

Lucifer continued, "So, when you came to the conference room at the satellite office of the Department of Worship, was it with every intention of following me as your new superior and starting to live out the ideas I presented to you?"

Again, Malachi hesitated.

"Come on, Malachi. It's a simple quest—"

"Yes, I did go with that intention. However, I didn't realize how far you were going to take it. As soon as I understood—"

Lucifer cut Malachi off, "Only answer the questions without the commentary. I think all here know now that you stepped over the line. You were no longer righteous in all your ways. You may have tried to backtrack later, but the truth is, you were as much a part of the rebellion as any of the rest of us."

"Wait, my King," pleaded Malachi, "as soon as I understood what I was doing would be a rebellion against You, I took a stand for You. I—"

"May I remind the court that the witness is to only answer my questions. You've already lectured me about adding commentary to my testimony. Please address the witness and let him know not to do the same."

Yeshua considered Lucifer's comments. Moments later, the Judge said, "Malachi, Lucifer is correct. You need to only answer his questions. Do not add narrative."

Laughter rose from the ranks of the Fallen as Malachi felt his face blush. Yeshua slammed his gavel. "Order, order!"

As the courtroom fell into a hush, Yeshua leaned forward. "Malachi, whose will do you seek first, My will or your own?"

Malachi could barely look his King in the eyes. "Your will, my Lord."

"Then, be still and at peace, and know I am God."

Malachi was broken and hurting. He knew he had allowed his heart and mind to go places they should never have gone. He wasn't certain where the delineation between questioning and rebellion was, but he knew he wanted no part in the latter. Now, more than ever, his deepest longing was to serve Elohim in exactly the way that best accomplished His will.

As Malachi contemplated the many places where he'd stumbled, Yeshua stopped him in mid-thought. "Malachi, you say My will is the motivation of your heart. Do you know how I am certain that is true?"

Malachi whispered, "Because You're omniscient? Because You're God?"

Lucifer jumped in and declared, "Who You are is not the question. Who Malachi is…well, that does matter. He was my Chief of Staff by choice, knowing full well that meant pursuing his own will ahead of Your will. He chose Self over You. No matter what he did thereafter, there is no doubt he became…how did you once describe me? Oh yes, he became 'one who is unclean' and all his 'righteous deeds are as filthy rags.' He condemns himself by his own testimony."

The heavenly host in the gallery began to murmur and groan. Members of the Fallen growled in protest. Several righteous angels looked accusingly at Malachi.

Gesturing to the crowd, Lucifer shouted out, "Does Elohim have a double-standard?"

Yeshua slammed down His gavel. "Silence, Son of Perdition! Are the true intentions of the heart defined by words or by deeds? Lucifer, you called Me Lord up to the Lost Day. Yet, the testimony clearly demonstrates that you were contemplating rebellion since mentoring Malachi, even in the days preceding that. You served Me with distinction, but you hungered for recognition, sought praise for yourself in the praise you generated for Me. Your words and deeds had all the appearance of righteousness. They demonstrate the difference between true devotion and the mere appearance of such.

"I am able to judge the thoughts and intentions of each heart. For a long time, your motivation has not been to praise and worship Me. For longer than you can even remember, it has been to serve yourself. Now your heart, and the heart of your followers, is hardened, bent only towards rebellion."

Yeshua pointed to Malachi. "Here is one who has faithfully served Me throughout His existence. I placed him in a position from which one-third of the heavenly host would have fallen. He entertained your ideas, and was tempted by your bribes. Yes, he chose to follow you in a sense. But where his initial words have the appearance of turning from Me, his actions in the Trade Room, on the battlefields, and in taking the stand today, knowing you would bring this attack against him, demonstrate where His heart was all along. He never left his loyalty to Me. His heart never hardened. He was never yours. He has always been Mine."

Yeshua looked at Malachi. "Who is your King, Lucifer or Me?

"You are and always will be my King."

"And whose will is more important to you, your own will or My will?"

"My desire is to see Your will done, now and forever."

Yeshua then declared, "I see into his heart and know this to be true. He walks in the light, as I am in the light. Therefore, we continue to have fellowship with one another. The same cannot be said for you, Lucifer, or any of the Fallen. He is Mine. You…you are not."

With that, the trial concluded and Elohim broke for deliberation. Once the verdict was read, Lucifer would have one final chance. His appeal.

******

Lucifer wracked his brain for a defense, some way to reverse course and avoid what seemed inevitable judgment. Even more, Lucifer still held out hope that there was a pathway to his deepest desire, to make himself *like the Most High*.

From the depths of his depravity, it came to him. An epiphany of sorts. *An avenue of escape. It might be the only one available to me, but I can see it. Who knew our salvation lay in the very nature of Elohim Himself?*

Lucifer needed to wait for exactly the right moment to present his argument, or rather, his accusation. *I can turn the tables on Elohim. This will be His trial, not mine. With all of the angels cowering in His presence, as they have never seen Him before, I can sway more angels to see Him for who He really is. Besides, I will never win this trial during normal arguments. My opportunity will come during the appeal phase of this trial. That's when I will turn this trial upside down.*

The court was called into recess to give Lucifer a break before he closed out his rebuttal to Yeshua's case.

******

Malachi and Corporal Joel sat, waiting for the court to be called back into session. As they did, they overheard two angels discussing the situation. Their conversation reminded them both just how unprecedented a time of upheaval they were experiencing in the heavens. Since the rebellion, a whole new set of words entered into the vocabulary of the heavenly places. They were strange words, and all seemed to carry a negative connotation.

Sin, War, Pain. Even Forgiveness and Justice implied shadowy counterparts.

By far the most disturbing words were those that referred to the condition and place which would forever be Lucifer and the Fallen's reality: Death and Hell.

The angel seated immediately to Malachi's left said, "Well, if none of us can have our lives ended, then what sentence could they possibly receive?"

His neighbor in the gallery leaned over and whispered, "One thing is certain. They can't stay here in the heavens. Their hearts are so hard, and they cannot be changed. There is simply no place for them in Elohim's perfect Presence."

"I guess they will have to be placed somewhere else," came a familiar voice from behind.

Malachi turned to look into the eyes of his supervisor, his mentor, his friend. "Barnabas!" he cried as the two angels nearly knocked their seats over in an attempt to embrace one another.

"Where have you been? Those captured by the Fallen during the rebellion were reintroduced into the community a long time ago. I feared the worst may have happened to you in the fray."

"The King decided you would maintain your focus more throughout the trial if you had a reason for righteous anger. He thought I might serve as added motivation."

Malachi whispered, "You are, more than you will ever know."

The two friends sat down and waited for the proceedings to continue. They couldn't help but overhear the conversation that continued between Malachi's neighbors in the gallery.

"Yes, everyone is now referring to living outside of the King's presence as 'Death' and the place where one would live in such a state as 'Hell.'"

"I can only imagine how . . .what's the word for it again?"

"Torturous. Horrible. There are a lot of new words for it."

"Oh yes… I can only imagine how horrible that must be. Everything good comes from Elohim. If He's not present there, then it must mean everything in Hell is…

"Bad. Horrible. I know. I can only imagine…"

Malachi leaned over to Corporal Joel and whispered, "You and I have some idea what it will be like."

"What do you mean?" replied Corporal Joel.

"Remember what things looked like at the Lake of Fire? Totally desolate. Burned beyond recognition."

"Sure."

"Well, I saw that area before it became that Lake of Fire. Elohim's glory shone down on it with an intensity I had never seen before. You know what? I think the King must have already been trying to cleanse the area, going all the way back to my mentorship. The cabin where Lucifer and I met was already falling apart as we convened there. I mean, the whole place creaked, but only when Lucifer was present. I think that place was being torn apart by Lucifer's..."

Malachi hesitated and then asked, "What are they calling actions done by someone that are less than perfect?"

"Sin. And since sins come out of the nature of the one doing them, those who act against Elohim's good, perfect and pleasing will are said to be Sinners."

"Oh yes, Sin. Sinners. I guess in the end, that area was so imperfect and covered by the effects of sin that it tore itself apart completely. All that remained was the Lake of Fire. And, you can see what effect it has on a celestial being."

"You mean Nergal, right?"

"Yes. Heard he was in the cabin when the ground opened up, and he fell into the Lake of Fire. Just a few moments, but that was enough to transform his appearance forever. They say even now he still feels the agonizing pain associated with his time in its flames. Still, Hell is supposed to be worse than even that." "I can only imagine." Malachi looked at the former Angel of Light and saw something he didn't think possible in the moment. He leaned over to Corporal Joel and whispered, "How, with the prospects of utter devastation, can Lucifer be so arrogant before the King? Not once has he tried to even hide his total contempt for Elohim."

******

Just before the court was called back into session, Lucifer looked around him and saw the faces of the angels who, like him, rebelled against God. He remembered the King's pronouncement against him during the trial, "By the abundance of your trade you were internally filled with violence, and you sinned." His mind wandered again to the conference room at Adramelech's office. It was there in the Trade Room that Lucifer promised things to the Fallen for which he neither possessed the power nor the authority to grant. In exchange, the Fallen had promised Lucifer a loyal army prepared to do whatever it took to oust Elohim from power and establish Lucifer as their new king.

While Lucifer remained confident that this would still eventually be the outcome, he could see in the solemn faces of his followers that they thought otherwise. When countless ages spent in the presence of Elohim's perfection, holiness, and absolute power had dulled them to the greatness of their King, they gave their reverence and loyalty to Lucifer. Now, their only reward for rebellion lay in whatever reality existed with Death and Hell.

As Lucifer looked more closely into their faces, he noticed that not all seemed full of fear. Many held anger and disdain. More still looked as though they wanted to destroy him as much as they wanted to take down the King. Lucifer had heard complaints when he was awaiting his trial, that they had risked the benefits of life with their Maker for Lucifer's "promised bribes." Now, none harbored expectations of a rise to power. In fact, they assumed the former Angel of Light was powerless before the One Who Is the Light.

Now, despite what Lucifer saw in their faces, he nodded to the Fallen reassuringly. It was time for his true defense. He spoke eloquently at first in hopes that he might still sway even more angels to his ideas. They had done their best to pull angels into their ranks, but the loss of Malachi stymied Lucifer's attempts to raise an even larger army. In the end, his followers were only able to recruit approximately one-third of the angels to join their rebellion. While still a huge number, it had left their forces outnumbered throughout the conflict.

******

Facing Elohim as the court returned to session, Lucifer continued his rebuttal. "Oh gracious King, You who are omniscient in all things. It is pointless for me to offer up a defense. As I am certain You alone know, I have struggled for some time now with how to ask for greater independence. When You spoke of creating this new being, man, I saw my chance at freedom slipping away. Surely, a wise King such as You must understand that an angel as glorious as I would eventually want to exercise my own will."

Elohim sternly interrupted, "How you have fallen, Oh star of the morning, son of the dawn. On the day I created you, you were blameless. Now, what is the unrighteousness I have found in you?"

"Surely Lord, it cannot be unrighteous for a celestial being to want to achieve more, and to be more," countered Lucifer. "You have had the freedom to do as you please throughout all of time, but we angels have had no such freedom. Certainly, You can see in me one who is Your equal in many ways. Give me my freedom, and I will promise to never act against You again. There is room enough for us each to be lord and king over our separate possessions."

Elohim responded, "I am the Lord, that is My name! I will not share My glory with another or the praise I deserve with false gods."

Unperturbed, Lucifer continued, "It is past time You promoted me to a position above all angels, to a title that represents my rightful seat of power. Even more, You should provide me with an opportunity to advance to a seat alongside You and Your Son, Yeshua."

Elohim glared at Lucifer. "To which of my angels did I ever say, sit at My right hand?"

"You feel You have done great and mighty things, but it is really we angels who have carried out Your bidding. You have ridden on our backs to the glory You enjoy. In fact, You have ridden on my back most of all. Were it not for our greatness, for my greatness as the true leader among the heavenly host, You wouldn't have a kingdom to rule at all."

Elohim's response was quick and simple. "Blessed are the poor in spirit, for theirs is the kingdom of heaven."

Lucifer's face turned red with anger. "That's just it. You want me to simply play my role as Your servant. You want me to accept being something less than who I am, to submit not just to you, but now to be little more than a slave to this new creature, man. My throne should be above every other created being, angel or man. I should be seated on the terrace of this Assembly alongside You and Yeshua. Have You not seen what I created in the first heaven? It is grander than anything You have here in Your kingdom. It is greater than anything You plan to create for this new creature, man. I demand to be made ruler over not just the heavenly host, but also mankind."

Elohim simply said, "'Blessed are the gentle in spirit, for they shall inherit the earth."

"Oh, so these creatures will live in a place called Earth." A sarcastic tone dripped from every word flowing from Lucifer's lips. "Well, when You look at all that I am, the radiance of my beauty and the eloquence of my words, why shouldn't I be their Overseer and Protector, as they are my servants? You unfairly withhold from me what is rightfully mine, a position akin to the Prince of Peace. Why not just withhold every blessing from me?"

"Blessed are those who hunger and thirst for righteousness, for they shall be satisfied. Blessed are the pure in heart, for they shall see God."

This so enraged Lucifer that he shouted, "How dare You punish me for being who I am? You created me better than all the rest, and perhaps as good as Yourself, and now You punish me for that magnificence. Where is the justice in that?"

CHAPTER TWENTY-FOUR

THE ACCUSER

"Be sober-minded; be watchful. Your adversary, the devil, prowls around like a roaring lion, looking for someone to devour."

1 Peter 5:8

Yeshua calmly looked at Lucifer, waiting to hear if he had any additional words in his defense. When nothing was presented, He slammed his gavel down and called an end to the initial proceedings. The Godhead Trinity then convened to determine how to proceed before calling the Heralding Angel over to receive Their decision. All who were present in the Assembly Chamber quietly waited for the verdict to be read.

"He who has ears, let him hear," announced the Heralding Angel. "Unrighteousness is based on being outside of the King's will. By desiring something different than what Elohim desires and acting in rebellion against His purposes, Lucifer and his followers will forever be called 'the Fallen.'" The herald waited for Yeshua to signal to proceed. When He did, the herald read the verdict, "In the eyes of God and this court, Lucifer and every Fallen angel are guilty of treason."

Frothing with indignation, Lucifer burst in, "This is unjust!" With all eyes upon him, he quickly composed himself. "You won't let me live the way I want to live. In fact, You won't let any of Your angels live as they desire. Why? Because You just want us to serve You and to do Your bidding. You make us nothing more than slaves, and if You create man and make us serve him as well, You will make us even less . . ." Lucifer stared intensely at the congregation of angels listening. "You will make us all slaves to slaves."

The Heralding Angel looked up at the King who simply nodded in his direction.

The herald continued to read from the scroll, "You demand to be independent from the King, but this is an impossible request. The reason He cannot give you independence from Him has many layers; however, there is one you most definitely have overlooked. By Him all things were created, both in the heavens and soon, the Earth, visible and invisible, whether thrones or dominions or rulers or authorities—all things have been created through Him and for Him. He is before all things, and in Him all things hold together. Lucifer, there is a way that seems right to a being, but it only brings that individual death. See. You and everything else are held together by the power of Elohim's will. Independence from Him is impossible, for there is nothing that exists outside of His sovereign hand.

"Furthermore, Lucifer, even if you could exist apart from Him, independence is not really what you seek. You want to be sovereign. Your hardened heart seeks to supplant the only true God and to usurp His throne. There can be no one else who is sovereign, for our King is and forever will be the Ruler of all things. Now, to the sentence our King is prepared to announce.

"You will be granted your independence from Elohim, at least to the extent that is even a possibility. However, rather than to find freedom in that independence, you will see what Elohim already knows. Your independence from Him will be your punishment for your acts of treason. Separation from Elohim for all eternity is not what you think it will be. Know this. Your independence from Him is your choice, as are the consequences which come with that decision. Like each of the other Fallen, you Lucifer, will have a chance to appeal the decision. But just as they found, it will be an exercise in futility."

The Herald continued, "There is a way that seems right to you. Elohim gave you free will so you could freely choose to worship and praise Him, to freely seek to do according to His good, perfect and pleasing will. You are free to choose otherwise, but to do so, to do that which is outside of Elohim's will, is to walk the path of imperfection. Since Elohim is perfect, it also means you are now incompatible with Him since you are no longer perfect. That which is imperfect is incompatible with that which is perfect, and therefore, that which is imperfect must be separated from perfection. You have chosen the path of Self. That path leads you away from the King based on your self-serving wills, but in the end, it would bring only eternal death."

Lucifer's heart sank within his chest, yet he quickly rebounded. He had one last remaining hope that he and his followers could somehow escape Death and Hell.

Yeshua said, "You have heard the sentence. What do you say, Lucifer?"

"I wish to appeal on behalf of myself and every angel who followed me." He hoped the result would mean more than just their salvation. Now was the time to see if he could flip the tables on the King and turn this into Elohim's trial rather than his own.

Lucifer looked into the faces of the Fallen. They gazed back with anticipation, as if hoping their king still had a defense that would reverse the damage caused by their failed rebellion.

Lucifer had been patient as long as he could. He thought, *Stay calm. All must see you standing for what is right. Now is the time to look like a sovereign king.*

He was certain he had a perfect plan. If presented properly, it would give Lucifer and the Fallen at least two chances to earn their freedom and perhaps demonstrate that the King was not worthy of His crown.

******

Lucifer remained kneeling as he brought his appeal, but rather than having his eyes down to the ground as most did when speaking to the King, Lucifer glared up at Elohim. "You say You are the Creator and that only You could do the things You accomplished in creating us all. Beyond that, however, have You really created anything else? Perhaps in creating us, You created beings who deserve to be treated at least as Your equals. You prove nothing in creating us without giving us the chance to independently demonstrate our own power and creativity."

"On the other hand, what I made in the Garden of Eden is as good as Your creation. All have seen what I did in the Garden when I took over as its Overseer. My work rivals Your own. I demand the opportunity to demonstrate that I am just as creative and powerful as You. Given the chance, I am certain I could accomplish more. In fact, I believe it will be clear that I can do more in living independently from You than I could ever achieve living in dependence upon You. When I demonstrate what I can do without Your constraints upon my freedom, all will recognize how repressed they have been. Then I have just as much right as You to pursue my own will and to have those who choose to follow me seek what they desire, instead of what You will."

In his heart, Lucifer added, *Soon, all will see me as a god worthy of their praise and worship. I will be Elohim's equal, at least until I present my second argument. Then, they will see I am actually greater than the King.*

A low rumble rippled through the Great Hall of the Assembly Chamber. Lucifer knew he had impacted both sides of the angelic host. *Perhaps, I can sway even more angels to support our cause. If Elohim has no one to follow Him, how will He maintain His claim to the crown and throne of heaven?*

Lucifer continued, moving on to his second, and from his perspective, strongest accusation. "You have also said You are perfect; in fact, perfection is the foundation for Your claim that You are God. The truth is that You really aren't perfect at all, which makes You nothing more than a liar and a tyrant. I can show that You, at the core of Your being, are a farce, or at best, a contradiction."

Several angels gasped at the statement, while members of the Fallen laughed and whispered their agreement.

Smiling, Lucifer stared confidently at Elohim. "You cannot be perfectly loving if You sentence all of us to an eternity of torment, pain, and suffering in Hell. If You are love in its perfect form as You claim, then that love is an agape love, an unconditional love. If it is unconditional, then You would find the way to spare us such torment. However, if we are really wrong in how we exercised our free will, if it really is unrighteous as You say, then to overlook our actions and spare us would, in itself, be something less than perfectly just. Therefore, You cannot be both perfectly loving and perfectly just at the same time. If You are not both traits at the same time, You are something less than perfect. If You are not perfect, then You are not God. If You are not God, You have no authority over me or any of those who follow me." He gestured to the others who had followed him on the Lost Day. "If You have no authority over us, then Your actions in condemning us are unjust. In fact, if You are acting unjustly, then it is not we who are on trial. It is You, Elohim, who is a tyrant and who is deserving of being cast out of the heavens. I am the one who is perfectly just in what I am doing."

All who were in the Assembly Chamber fell silent. All looked at Elohim to see how the King would react to the accusations being leveled by Lucifer. Some began whispering to one another that there was logic in what Lucifer was saying. Would Elohim meet this challenge? Could He? If not, could He really be considered God?

Lucifer readied himself to continue his rebellion; he felt reinvigorated despite the sentence already pronounced against him. He smiled at the Fallen and again whispered to himself, "I will make myself be like the Most High God."

Lucifer knew accusing God was a bold move, but he also felt certain the King would not allow an accusation to remain unanswered if such could, in any way, diminish His glory. Lucifer thought, *Elohim can't allow my accusations to stand. They must be addressed. I will show all that I am His equal. I can duplicate the King's work in creation.* He reasoned, *I cross-bred plants on my own without the King's help. Given enough time, I'm sure I could create a heaven and all that resides within it that is just as magnificent as anything Elohim creates. All I would need is enough TIME.*

Lucifer watched as the herald stepped back to receive a second parchment from Yeshua. As the angel stepped forward to the front of the terrace once again, he did so to silence. All had been waiting for this moment. The question was, would Elohim carry through on His earlier sentence, or would He adjust His decision based on this accusation against His essence and His character? What would be the eternal destiny of Lucifer and the Fallen?

The herald began, "Hear this decree and summary judgment. On the counts of treason against Lucifer and the entire list of participants in the rebellion on the day now referred to as the 'Lost Day,' the King finds them all guilty as charged. As a result, Lucifer and any of his followers who had access to the Holy Mount are hereby banished from the Highest Heaven forevermore. Furthermore, they shall be isolated for a time in the smallest possible space in the first heaven while the rest of the heavens are cleansed from the defilement brought upon it by Lucifer and the Fallen. Once all has been cleansed, these rebels will be expelled forever from the heavenly places. This expulsion from every level of the heavenly places will be for all eternity.

As such, the new level of heaven, what will henceforth be called the first heaven, and all it contains shall serve as a place of exile where they shall await such time as the King determines to answer the accusations made by Lucifer.

"Henceforth, Lucifer shall forfeit his name and his title. No longer will he be known as Lucifer; no longer will he be a Guardian Cherub; and no longer will he be referred to as the 'Angel of Light.' Instead, he will be referred to among the angelic host as 'Satan,' which means the Accuser and Adversary. This seems fitting for one who accuses God and contends against Him as the leader of the Fallen. No longer will Satan and his Fallen be allowed to come to the highest heavens, except by the request of or as permission is granted by our King."

"The duration of this exile to the lowest heaven will be at the discretion of the King based on His wisdom and foreknowledge. It shall be for such a time as is appropriate for all of Lucifer's accusations to be addressed and for all to agree that Elohim alone is God and King. The period of exile will demonstrate the false nature of the accusations leveled by Satan and the reality of Elohim's deity and sovereignty. Following this period of exile, Satan and the Fallen will face the terms of the original sentence—eternal separation from the King in the lake of fire found in that place known as 'Hell.'"

Cheers of elation went up from the ranks of the Fallen who were certain they were destined for immediate damnation. Lucifer saw anything that ended without he and the Fallen being sent immediately to Hell as certain victory. Though uneasy cheers were heard from the Faithful Host, they also wondered at what the King hoped to achieve from this ruling. Yet, they remained steadfast in their belief that the King's thoughts were higher than their thoughts, and His ways higher than their ways. Despite Lucifer's accusations, it seemed they would trust the King to know what was best and appropriate to the situation.

The Heralding Angel continued, "Once again, these rebellious actions are considered a desecration of that which has always been holy. The King now orders the cleansing of all areas touched by these rebels since the moment such thoughts of rebellion entered their minds."

While preparations were made for cleansing the spiritual realm, Satan and the Fallen were prepared for their expulsion from the heavenly places.

CHAPTER TWENTY-FIVE

BANISHED

"And you sinned; Therefore, I have cast you as profane
from the mountain of God, and I have destroyed you, O covering
cherub, from the midst of the stones of fire."
Ezekiel 28:16b

With the trial finished, the judgment rendered, and the punishment declared, Satan and the Fallen were brought to a location in the lowest heaven just east of the Garden of Eden. The unrighteous nature of their treacherous column of fallen angels left a trail of defiled space behind them as they marched to the location designated by Elohim. This defiled space, as well as anywhere else in the six levels of heaven, would have to be cleansed as soon as possible. But first, Satan and the Fallen would need to be addressed. All knew there was no place in the heavens for this unholy throng.

So holy is Elohim that He cannot tolerate wickedness. His eyes are too pure to even look at anything that is the slightest bit unholy. He and anything that is imperfect in any way are simply incompatible.

Satan and the Fallen were the embodiment of depravity and sinfulness. It was therefore Michael and the other Archangels who marched Satan and his followers to the place where their exile would begin, where the Fallen would await Elohim's response to Satan's accusations.

When they all arrived at the location designated by the King, it was no different than any other spot in the lowest level of heaven. However, this would be the point from which Yeshua, at the direction of Yahweh, would deal with the unholy presence of those who committed treason against the King.

Once again, Elohim's actions would be multi-faceted in their purposes. The banishment of Satan and the Fallen would do more than just expel the impurity of their sin from the King's presence. That new level of heaven would become the physical universe in which Elohim would place His greatest creation, mankind. Through them, He would put to rest the accusations on which Satan and the Fallen now placed all of their hope.

To begin this work, a Heralding Angel read back excerpts from the trial. Though the statements provided for each of the condemned were slightly different, they all followed the same common theme. Each member of the Fallen, including Satan, commented on their desire to exist independently from the King. All acknowledged by verbal attestation that they remembered making the statement, they agreed with the statement, and they still wanted to live independently from Elohim. With this, the herald stepped back and waived Michael forward to carry out the sentences.

Michael and the Archangels, along with Malachi and Corporal Joel, who participated due to their efforts on the Lost Day, herded Satan and the Fallen to the location designated by the King. Once they arrived, Yeshua appeared on the scene in a white robe, clothed in the purity of His righteousness, showered in the glory of Yahweh, and immersed in the Cloud-like form of the Holy Spirit. Yeshua looked at the condemned and saw nothing but disdain and arrogance written across their faces. Even though facing eternal separation from their Creator and Sustainer for their treasonous acts, the desire to live independently from the King, no matter how high the cost, drove their rebellious hearts onward.

Yeshua held both hands out as if He was gathering His enemies into one great embrace. As He did so, He spoke to the rest of His angelic host. "Not everyone who says to Me, 'Lord, Lord,' is one of My servants; but he who does the will of My Father, who is worshipped from the Holy Mount to the Garden of Eden, these belong to Me. Satan and his Fallen have said to Me since the moment I created them, 'Lord, Lord, have we not served Thee, have we not praised Thee, and have we not worshipped Thee.' But now, unrighteousness has been found in their hearts. They now serve, praise, and worship themselves. They no longer remember who I am; they no longer want to know Me."

He lifted His hands high into the air and brought them together in a tight ball. "My faithful host, those fallen angels who stand before us have practiced wickedness and lawlessness in My holy kingdom. Not only this, they desire to live apart from Me. I will give them what they desire until such time as I execute My final judgment against them for their unrighteousness and sin against Me."

With His hands clasped together, He looked down at Satan and the Fallen and declared in a loud voice, "There is no longer a place for you in heaven."

A fiery whirlwind descended, as if launched directly from the Holy Mount. At once, the fallen angels were caught up in the chaotic winds and lifted high into the air. Though they spun about faster and faster, instead of flying apart, they were pulled together into a tight funnel.

In much the same way, the defiled portions of the higher heavens were caught in the chaotic fire and winds and drawn together with the Fallen. Massive amounts of celestial matter collapsed in on itself until it became hard to distinguish the fallen angels from the mass of debris.

Powerful centrifugal forces countered by the will of the living God produced an enormous amount of heat as the Fallen and the corrupted debris were drawn into an ever-tightening tornado. Yeshua then held His clasped hands in front of Him for all the angelic host to see.

The spinning mass of fallen angels collapsed into a sphere with each revolution. Soon, Yeshua was actually able to lay hold of the swirling mixture of bodies and debris, first in two hands, and then in just one. As He did, the mass of bodies and debris formed into an infinitely dense singularity. Again, in a loud voice, Yeshua declared, "I will cast them from My kingdom into a furnace of fire, in that place, there will be weeping and gnashing of teeth."

Around the swirling ball, a dense layer of pure matter formed from nothingness. Inside, the mass of fallen angels continued to pick up speed. Centrifugal forces continued to grow, yet rather than bursting out, the sphere continued to collapse inwardly on itself. Satan and the Fallen found it impossible to open their eyes due to the agonizing flames and heat which engulfed their entire bodies. Temperatures were so high that light was unable to glow, leaving each fallen angel in complete darkness, despite being engulfed in flames. The pain was indescribable, though it lasted only for an infinitesimal fraction of a moment. Still, in that instant the corrupted matter within the singularity was purified in the fires that lay within. That was when the true Power behind the expulsion of Satan and his followers took over.

Yeshua raised his clenched fist in the air. Indeed, the King had created a furnace in which the fallen angels had been cast. Wails and screams echoed from within the singularity, from within the clenched fist of Yeshua. He then said, "I now commit them to the darkness where they will be reserved for the final judgment."

The faithful angels present for the expulsion of the Fallen looked on in guarded wonder. Never before had they witnessed the King carrying out a sentence against a sinful being, and never before had they seen a new level of heaven created.

Now, they watched as a third of their original number experienced the King's wrath against sin. As they looked on, Yeshua's fist began to pulsate with the radiance of His glory. His voice boomed, "Depart from Me you who practice lawlessness and unrighteousness in My holy abode, for I never knew you." He cast the singularity away and watched as a new gateway formed beneath them. Not since the creation of the six current levels of heaven had the spiritual realm experienced the outpouring of the omnipotence of Elohim. The energy behind the expulsion of the Fallen transferred to the tiny singularity, which then shattered as it exited what was now the second level of heaven to form the spiritual and physical realms of a new level of heaven. The first heaven was born, and with it, the physical universe which would one day be observed by mankind—scientist and layman alike.

******

With a defiant glare back into the heavens at Yeshua, Satan shook his fist at the King and shouted out loudly for all to hear, "Mark my words; given the chance now to live independently from Elohim, I will achieve far more than I ever did when forced to serve Him as His slave. My followers, we will show the King to be nothing more than an oppressive, powerful tyrant. Not only that, but I will prove the King is not God after all. I will show that He is not perfect."

In a last word, Satan declared the battle cry which he had spoken on the way to the Assembly Chamber on the Lost Day. It was these words which stood out to Yahweh and allowed Him to know the timing was right to draw out the rebelliousness in Satan's heart. Now the words which would be captured in the Great Book in *Isaiah 14: 13-14* rolled off his tongue once more, declaring his intention to one day climb each of the seven levels of heaven to take the throne he still believed was better suited to his control:

I will ascend to heaven;
I will raise my throne above the stars of God;
I will sit on the mount of the assembly;
I will ascend above the heights of the clouds;
And finally,
I will make myself like the Most High
Yeshua raised his hands, and while Satan's lips continued to move, no sound

was heard. The King calmly responded, "You will have your opportunity to prove your words. Know this, everything which transpires in the first level of heaven will, in the end, be to My glory and to your condemnation. You will try to duplicate what I do, but all will see that apart from Me, you can do nothing. All will see that I alone am God. I Am the I Am." With that, Yeshua walked away from the portal between the first heaven and the second heaven.

The Heralding Angel stepped forward, unrolled a scroll, and declared, "No member of the Fallen may enter the heavens above without first being granted access by our King. There are no exceptions to this proclamation." With that, the portal was sealed, and Guardian Angels were placed on duty to prevent any attempted reentry by Satan or his followers.

******

As time was now measured in a trillionth of a billionth of a trillionth of a second, the singularity containing Satan and the Fallen burst forth into their place of exile. Crashing across the universe, members of the Fallen, and the matter contained within the singularity's shell, were scattered in all directions. As the fallen angels came to rest, they looked back to see what became of their comrades. When they did, all were drawn to a magnificent light in the distance. Using that light as a beacon, the fallen angels made their way towards its glow. This was to be their sanctuary, and for a brief moment in eternity, Satan's kingdom. It would remain such until the time arrived for Satan's accusations to be addressed by the King. Until then, this would be their kingdom...even though to Elohim and the heavenly host, it was little more than a trash heap. It would not always be viewed as such.

CHAPTER TWENTY-SIX

COUNTERFEIT SPLENDOR

"Your heart was lifted up because of your beauty;
You corrupted your wisdom by reason of your splendor."
Ezekiel 28:17a

13.77 Billion Years Ago as some estimate time;
6000 years ago according to others. Regardless...moments before
"In the beginning, God created the heavens"
...moments before the first trillionth of a billionth
of a trillionth of a second of the new heaven
...moments before "Inflation"

T he pain pulsing through Satan's body was excruciating. Screams of agony were all around, and even within him. Invisible flames swirled about, filling his lungs and penetrating into his closed eyes. There was no relief from the immeasurably hot temperatures. If that wasn't bad enough, the smell of the bodies burning around him made Satan nauseated. All of his senses were bombarded in an instant...except for his sight. He dared not open his eyes again. The last time he tried, it did him no good anyway. All was utterly dark within the singularity. So overwhelming was his suffering, he actually caught himself praying, "Elohim...make it end. Set me free from this torture." He stopped himself...*Oh yes, He doesn't care about me any longer. He never really did. I'm being tossed aside like that dirty rag He called me. Used and discarded.*

Then, in less than an instant, it all changed. Suddenly, he felt everything around him unwind. His breath rushed from his lungs, and for a moment, he couldn't inhale. Seconds later, Satan found himself floating in dead space, completely alone. Despite the excruciating pain which forced him to close his eyes when they were within the singularity, the dead silence of his current surroundings beckoned to him to chance a look around. Slowly and fearfully, he opened his eyes. There was absolutely nothing. Then, the former Angel of Light made a significant discovery...

Look at how brightly my glory shines against this great darkness. Elohim was never this magnificent. He screamed, "Who is like the Lord our God, the One who sits enthroned on high? I know the answer...I am like the Mo..."

"I would say, 'You are like the Lord our God, the Most High.'" It was the familiar voice of Adramelech as he interrupted Satan's praise to himself, "In fact, I would say you are even greater still, but I have always believed that to be the case."

"Adramelech, good to see you. Can you believe a loving God would put anyone through such suffering? How is that possible?"

Adramelech answered, "Tyrant."

Suddenly, two more angels appeared. Then another, and another...Eventually, Satan couldn't believe his eyes as a mighty army formed out of the darkness surrounding him.

"How did you all find me?" asked Satan.

"That's easy," answered Adramelech. "We all spirit leaped to the location of your glorious appearing. Your radiance is overwhelmingly bright here in this new heaven. Actually, most of us feel you rival even Elohim here in our new abode."

Satan thought about it for a second. Finally, he said, "Many of you feared for your eternity during our trial and sentencing. Understand who I am and what I have accomplished on your behalf. Do you still live under a tyrant's heel?"

"No!" yelled Adramelech and the Fallen together.

"Are you now able to freely pursue your own will?"

The Fallen all yelled in unison, "Yes!"

"And, am I not now free to act as your king in every respect?"

Without hesitation, the jubilant crowd yelled, "Yes! All hail our new eternal king."

Satan said, "We might not have taken the kingdom from the King, but we forced the King to give us our independence. To grant you a new king, and me a kingdom. I believe, given the numerical superiority of our enemies and the presence of Elohim on their side, anyone who observed what transpired on the Lost Day could see a victory on our part. Now, we will make our Kingdom be something grander than His own. He will be forced soon to admit that I am in every way His equal."

Adramelech cried, "To Satan be all glory and honor and power and praise both now and forevermore."

Satan said in a loud voice, "Since our trial, Elohim has called me 'Satan, the Accuser.' I believe a different name is more fitting for who I am. Call me 'Beelzebub, the Destroyer.' By my hand, I will destroy all that He adores. Gaze upon my glory and know that your King will be more than a conqueror in the power of Self. Gaze upon my splendor."

With that, Satan rose above his followers, emitting a beautiful mixture of brilliant colors across the empty space that was their new home. The fallen angels could not recall seeing this before in the higher heavens. As he did, many below him shouted in a loud voice, "There is none like King Beelzebub. To him be all praise now and forever. Who can extinguish his glory? None. All hail King Beelzebub."

******

"Did you hear that?" called one of the Guardian Angels stationed at the new portal to the lowest heaven in which the Fallen were banished.

Malachi rushed over.

"Hear what?" answered Corporal Joel, instinctively following close behind.

"I could have sworn I just heard screaming from the lower heaven, but how is that even possible?" said the Guardian Angel. "Isn't the new heaven supposed to be completely detached from the higher heavens?"

The three angels stood silently for a moment, listening intently at the portal. "There it is again. Did you hear it that time?" asked the Guardian Angel.

"Yes, but it didn't sound like they were upset. It sounded like a celebration," said Corporal Joel.

"I'm with you. How is it possible to hear into that level of heaven when it is supposed to be completely separate from the higher heavens?" asked the second Guardian Angel assigned to the portal.

From behind them came the familiar voice of the Archangel Michael saying, "Do you not recall how the levels of heaven work? Each level has a physical and a spiritual component. The spiritual of the lower is in the physical of the higher. Their primary essence is in the physical realm of the newly formed heaven. That means their residual selves are in the spiritual realm of their heaven, but none of their primary essence exists in our physical realm. What you are hearing is their residual presence in the lower heaven's spiritual realm."

Malachi and Corporal Joel turned to face the one with whom they fought back-to-back on the Lost Day. The Archangel Michael stepped from within one of the guard towers overlooking the portal to the first level of heaven. Corporal Joel quickly came to attention and gave salute.

"At ease Corporal. I just came to see this new portal for myself and to check on the early guard detail, see if they need any assistance." Michael then added, "Unfortunately, we may have to listen to them for a while."

Satan cried out, "You may have power in your heavens, but this space is mine. I am more powerful and more radiant than You in my kingdom. Can you not see, here my splendor is above yours, Elohim?"

After several minutes of listening to the enemies of God reveling in what they viewed as a victory on their part, the Archangel Michael cried out, "How long, O LORD? How long will the wicked be allowed to gloat? How long will they speak with arrogance? How long will these evil ones boast?"

Unexpectedly, Yeshua appeared in their midst and said, "Let those who are wise boast not of their wisdom, nor those who are strong boast of their strength, nor the one who is rich boast of his riches, but let him who boasts boast of this, that he knows and understands Me."

Pointing toward the portal where Satan was banished, Yeshua said, "This one who should know Us so well, does not know Us at all anymore and neither do We know him."

Yeshua looked the three heroes of the Lost Day in the eye and softly said, "When pride comes, then comes dishonor. Behold now, I have stretched out my hand against him, and I shall diminish his portion."

Satan yelled, "What can you do to me now, King? In my Kingdom, there is no place for You. Your eyes are too pure to behold iniquity. I am untouchable. You can't even come into my Kingdom. You are powerless against me now."

Again, Michael, Malachi, and Corporal Joel begged Yeshua to put an end to the taunts against Him, but He only raised His hand, calling for silence.

As the taunts of the fallen angels against their Creator continued, Yeshua said, "Everyone who is proud of heart is an abomination to me; assuredly, they will not go unpunished."

He then drew the attention of His loyal angels to the most insignificant of particles floating throughout space in the newly created universe. While it was small, it seemed to be what the light of Satan's glory and that of the other fallen angels were using to actually illuminate the darkness. Yeshua then said, "Behold, I have made everything for its purpose." Pointing to some particles with His right hand, He slowly closed His fist as if He was grabbing them tightly.

Immediately, fallen angels began to complain about the temperature quickly rising to unbearable levels. At the same time, the radiance of the fallen angels began to diminish until only Satan's glory remained.

Satan angrily raised his fist to the heavens and yelled, "You cannot harm me if you are to truly prove me wrong in my accusations. Attack me if you will, but you will only be showing Yourself to be the tyrant I know you to be."

Yeshua then said to the three angels at his side, "I am the LORD; that is my name! I will not yield my glory to another or my praise to a false god." With that, Yeshua quickly blew into His clenched fist. When He did, the glory of Satan went out, leaving him and his fallen angels in complete darkness. The only evidence that the Fallen still remained in their place of exile came in their screams for mercy from the heat which eliminated the light.

From out of the darkness, Satan screamed, "Again, You seek only after Your own will regardless of the suffering You cause to Your servants. You hold us back from being all we can be. You are nothing more than a tyrant, and someday, I will show that again. We will overcome, and I will rise above You. When I do, there will be no end to Your own torment. Mark my words, You will see me again, and I will destroy everything You hold dear." At last, Yeshua closed his hand and Satan's distant voice went silent.

CHAPTER TWENTY-SEVEN

THE CALLING

"I thank him who has given me strength, Christ Jesus our Lord,
because he judged me faithful, appointing me to his service…"
1 Timothy 1:12

Malachi was surprised when he received the invitation to come to the Mount of the Assembly for a meeting with Yeshua and the Archangel Michael. Since his involvement on the Lost Day and at the trials of the Fallen, he had been included in numerous discussions with higher sphere angels. Still, to be included with Yeshua as well was special for any angel at any level.

When Malachi walked into the Great Hall, the Archangel Michael was already sitting on the front row. High above him on the Terrace overlooking the Great Hall, sat Yeshua.

"Oh great, you're here. We can get started now," said Michael upon seeing Malachi entering the chamber.

Yeshua seemed pleased to have two of what had proven to be his best warriors in the room with Him. It didn't take long for Yeshua to get to His point.

"Michael and Malachi. We've discussed on numerous occasions just how special the two of you are and will be going forward. Both of you were created for very specific purposes, not the least of which were military strategy and tactics. Now that we are on the verge of an even greater war with Satan and the Fallen, we are ready to place you in positions to take advantage of your supernatural gifts.

"Let me start with you Michael. You were created with a special skill set; one you didn't know you had until the situation arose which called for those skills to be exercised. We will be creating the Department of Celestial Warfare to provide oversight for the Army of the Host across every theater of battle in every level of heaven. Will you accept the title of Primecerius over that Department and take on that role?"

Michael bowed his head. "I would be honored."

Yeshua then turned to Malachi and said, "And you. You were created to be 'the One' who would walk beside Lucifer as he fell from being the Angel of Light to Satan, the Accuser. You have witnessed just about every major event involving My Angelic Host as well as the creation of the new level of heaven, the universe in which I will one day place Earth. Those eyewitness experiences have given you unique insights which go far beyond those of the rest of the angelic host. It will be important for you to share these insights with your comrades and, someday, with mankind."

Malachi bowed. "Blessed beyond measure…I would be honored to do so, my King."

"Thank you, Malachi. There is one more task for you to perform. We gave you special skills in the area of combat. We want you to train our warriors in both the fighting skills and the background story associated with creation. Please report to Camp Wisdom to begin serving as a Cohort Trainer for the Army of the Host. Of course, you will have a rank within the Army of the Host…Lieutenant. Congratulations…just know there will be many battles with Satan and the Fallen going forward. Train our warriors well. Eternity is at stake for the Sons of God and Sons of Men."

With that, both Primecerius Michael and Lieutenant Malachi knelt before their King as Yeshua made His exit. When they arose, Michael said, "Well, I guess you now report ultimately to me through my command structure since all New Warrior Training Camps are within the Department of Celestial Warfare."

Malachi snapped to attention.

"At ease, Lieutenant. I mentioned that because I know you are very close with Barnabas back at the Department of Celestial Fellowship. I suggest you don't forget to speak with him before reporting to Camp Wisdom. You've seen the good and bad of mentorship. Give honor to whom honor is due. I would suggest you head to your new quarters, but not before you stop by Barnabas' residence."

"Why is that, Sir?" replied Malachi.

"I might have let slip what was taking place here today. No details. Just let him know he might not be seeing you nearly as much as in the past. So, go on. Tell him why all the fuss. Just don't take too long. We need you to start immediately. We have an army to build."

Malachi saluted and made his way to the exit. This time, he had no reservations about the new position he had to share with his mentor and friend.

******

As the new lieutenant walked along the street called Adonai on his way to Barnabas' residence, he found himself praising Elohim as he'd never done before. Always in the past, he worshipped the King for His nature and for His wondrous acts in creation. But now, he found himself looking on the beauty around him with even greater appreciation. *To think, had Satan won, we might have lost all of this. Praise to Elohim for being a shield against evil and for His power to maintain the perfection of His celestial creation.*

Malachi shook his head, remembering just how close he'd come to missing out on this beauty and majesty forever. He bowed his head and prayed, "Lord, Your greatness is unsurpassed. You not only create all things by the power of Your will, but You sustain them as well, even in the face of great adversity. Truly, You are the One and Only God. Thank you for saving me even when it appeared I would turn my back on you. You are so faithful."

******

To Malachi's surprise, the door to Barnabas' quarters was ajar when he arrived. Within, he could hear two familiar voices. "Is that you, Malachi?" asked Barnabas just as his star associate knocked on the door.

"How did you know? I wasn't even planning to come," answered Malachi.

"Well, it may have not been your original plan, but it was Ruach Elohim's." Corporal Joel grabbed his friend by the shoulder and pulled him inside. As he did, Malachi noticeably winced.

"You, too? It still burns everywhere I was struck on the Lost Day. I don't understand it. Everyone else seems to have gotten over their injuries, but I still have that burning sensation in each of my wounds."

"Actually, you two aren't the only ones. Everywhere they struck me still hurts. I wonder why we three are like this?" asked Barnabas.

"You always told me the King was open to our questions," said Malachi. "Let's just ask Him."

With that, the three angels of God bowed their heads in prayer. They prayed for healing. They prayed for understanding. They prayed most of all that the King's will would be done in the situation. When they lifted their heads and opened their eyes, they found themselves engulfed in the swirling cloud of Ruach Elohim.

In a soft yet authoritative voice, Ruach Elohim addressed the petition. He began, "Your prayer has been heard. I know the plans I have for you. Plans to prosper you. To give you hope and a future. For now, I must say no to your request for healing."

"May we ask why?" asked Barnabas. "It seems such a reasonable request. All others who were injured defending You on the Lost Day have since returned to perfect health. Yet we three who defended you so staunchly and who suffered so greatly in that cause remain in such pain."

Ruach Elohim answered, "Before the Lost Day, there was praise, there was worship, there was thanksgiving. All was radiance and glory, for in all, there was perfection. But now, since the Lost Day, there is Satan and the Fallen, and there is an accusation to address. We will not allow this to continue forever, but only until such time as none doubt Our sovereignty and preeminence. In the end, every knee will bow, in heaven, on Earth, and even those under the Earth. As long as time has any meaning, there will be a time to heal and a time for pain. For now, for the sake of your brothers-in-arms, this is a time for pain for you."

The three angels looked at one another, puzzled expressions betraying their continued lack of understanding.

Undisturbed by their sustained concerns, Ruach Elohim said, "In Our presence, all things are made new. Every pain and injury is healed, every tear wiped away, all guilt removed, and every memory which disrupts perfect worship from taking place is expunged. All is cast into the Sea of Forgetfulness. Everything that detracts from perfect worship will be no more."

Corporal Joel whispered, "I don't understand. You're saying all pain is removed in Your presence, and yet, You purpose us to continue to suffer. Why?"

Barnabas added, "I already made myself weak so that your strength could be displayed all the more. There is no need for me to continue to suffer like this. In my life, that point is already made."

Ruach Elohim prodded Malachi's heart so softly, it seemed like a whisper. He sensed the Holy Spirit say, "You are the One. Proclaim understanding."

Barnabas and Corporal Joel looked to Malachi for an explanation they knew would still fall short of providing a logical rationale for what they were being asked to go through.

Where once there was confusion, all gave way to perfect clarity. Malachi said, "Time. There is a time to create, and a time to cleanse. There is a time to build up, and a time to tear down. In the presence of the King; however, there is only perfection. Perfect praise, perfect worship, perfect health, perfect peace. In that perfection, before the glory and majesty of our King, how could a memory such as the Lost Day remain at all? How could they even recall Satan and the Fallen? How could anyone even remember the horrors of warfare when this must be remembered in the future? A fight still remains."

Malachi looked at Ruach Elohim and said, "You need us to remember. Our pain will allow us to do so. You are asking us to continue to suffer so that we will remember and be able to teach others about it before they enter the coming battle."

"It is a thorn in your side, but it has a purpose. Are you willing to accept this calling?"

Barnabas answered without hesitation, "Of course, my King."

Joel added, "I live for Your glory. My delight is in You. Your will be done." Ruach Elohim drew close to Malachi, waiting for his response.

For a moment, the lieutenant stood in silence, contemplating exactly how he would respond. Finally, and with conviction, he said, "I consider our present suffering not worth comparing with the glory which will be revealed in us. There will come a time when all of creation will groan with pain until that day when You determine to put an end to Satan's accusations once and for all. If our current suffering shortens that time even for a minute, then I gladly accept that calling. May Thy will be done once and for always."

EPILOGUE

EARTH, THE LOWEST LEVEL
OF HEAVEN: PRESENT DAY

Across the camp, the most recent graduates from Camp Wisdom remained in complete silence. They had always wondered at the pain their commanders seemed to be in during the course of boot camp. They thought perhaps it was because of this continued pain that these supposed heroes from the Lost Day trained new warriors rather than themselves being warriors on the frontline fight against Satan and the Fallen. They now understood.

Gideon looked at Lieutenant Malachi with shame in his eyes. "You've endured so much for so long. He asked and you obeyed, knowing how great the suffering would be, but with no idea how long it would continue."

"I did so because I consider myself as the weakest of all warriors. I nearly rebelled. I almost declared my allegiance to Satan. Perhaps even now, I deserve to be where they are."

Gideon replied, "If only I would one day be found as faithful."

"You will do even more. Just remember, you can do all things through Elohim. He will strengthen you."

Malachi stood before the cohort for all to see. As he did, he shouted, "Now you have heard the tale from the beginning. Yes, mankind brings much suffering, but they were not the start of our present darkness. It was our kind who introduced darkness where once there was only light. It is our responsibility to restore the Light of Life, or at least to live out the calling Elohim has placed on us to play our part as He restores the Light. You can do all things through Our great King who strengthens You. Have no more doubts. You are ready. You are more than conquerors through Yeshua. He has won the victory. It is ours to claim. Make straight the way of His return as He reclaims the lower heavens."

All stood as one and cheered. As they did, Malachi tried to slide out as secretly as he had arrived. Just as Lieutenant Malachi stepped beyond the view of the cohort, Corporal Gideon caught him by the arm.

"Sir, I know we are more than conquerors through Yeshua. Mankind is as well, and yet, from what I hear, we continue to lose ground in the minds of men. So many die each day without the hope that comes in the sacrifice of Yeshua. We may ultimately win this war, but each battle sees more and more men and women losing their eternities. We need to do more. I want to do more."

Malachi placed a hand on Gideon's shoulder and whispered, "So do I."

******

The Primecerius Michael stood in the War Room of the Department of Celestial Warfare. He shook his head as he read the most recent report related to the current beliefs of yet another generation of men. He read: Percent of mankind who claim to believe in the existence of a Creator God…down from 79% to 71%.

Percent of mankind who profess to be atheist, agnostic or non-affiliated with any religious belief…up from 16% to 23%.

Percent of mankind in the latest generation who profess to be atheist, agnostic, or non-affiliated with a religious belief…34%.

Projected percent of mankind in the next generation who profess to be atheist, agnostic, or non-affiliated with a religious belief…48% up to 58%.

Michael handed the report to an aide and said, "Burn it. We have to do better."

Looking back as he left the office, the aide said, "Sir, Lieutenant Malachi is here in the hallway waiting for you."

"Send him in…Malachi, how long have you been waiting? Just knock next time."

"I needed a moment."

"For what?"

Lieutenant Malachi walked over to the map of the lowest heaven. Across the globe, more and more men and women were giving into the enemy's lies. Universities that once upheld the message of the Great Book used by the King to reveal Himself to mankind now openly promoted its inaccuracies. From all appearances, the Earth looked the opposite of the higher heavens on the Lost Day. Red dots now outnumbered the green dots by a considerable number, and the trends aren't improving.

"I just left my last cohort in the field. They were caught in an ambush just one day removed from boot camp. The enemy is gaining ground on every front. We need to do more. Souls are on the line."

Michael nodded, "You're right. We'll double the pace of new cohort training. We need more angels in the field to influence the direction of mankind's thinking. We need to mold their presuppositions more effectively."

Malachi walked up to the map just in time to see another green dot fade and then return as bright red. He turned to Michael and said, "No, it's not just that we need more angels in the field. We need more angels who fought on the Lost Day...who were there from the very beginning."

Michael grinned, "And who do you think should join our warriors in the field, Lieutenant?"

"There are others who are now able to train a new cohort for the field," answered Malachi.

"The field needs more of us who know already the sting of battle, the tricks of the enemy, and the focus it takes to win a heart to the message of our King. I can stand it no longer. I need to be on the front lines. I need to go back into this battle."

Primecerius Michael picked up another report from his desk. His heart sank as he read of even more losses in the field. Drawing his flaming sword from its sheath, he set the file on fire and watched as it burned down to a small shred. He turned to face Malachi and said, "You're right. Time for you to join this battle. Gather a few angels you believe can make a difference and have them help you train the next cohort for the field. The next time one of your cohorts leaves Camp Wisdom, you and your leadership will leave with them. As I recall, we are calling this next group Genesis Cohort."

"Thank you, Sir. We can stem the tide. They just need to hear the truth from someone who was there. Ruach Elohim said there is a time for war and a time for peace. I have spent more than enough time in relative peace. This is my time for war."

"Then assemble your leadership team and report back to Camp Wisdom. This time, you train your own cohort. Go quickly, with all blessings."

As Malachi began to close the door, he suddenly stopped and peeked back in.

"Yes, lieutenant? Did you forget something?"

"Yes, Sir. Just wanted to say thank you. I am truly Blessed Beyond Measure." With that he left the room and headed to the portal which exited at the front entrance of Camp Wisdom. As he did, he whispered to himself, "Genesis Cohort. Time to face my old mentor. Time to restore the *Heavens and the Earth.*"

ABOUT THE SERIES

QUESTIONS FOR DISCUSSION

Created: The Devil's Apprentice – Book One

The story of God's angels from the perspective of one of their own, from their creation, through their rebellion, and on to their subsequent banishment prior to the Creation account found in the Book of Genesis, Chapter One.

Major Questions Addressed:

1. Why would an omniscient God who is perfect in every way ever choose to create the angels?
2. Why did God not just condemn Satan and the fallen angels immediately to Hell following their rebellion against Him?
3. How does the fall of the angels tie into the creation of our universe and the Earth?

Created: Heaven and Earth – Book Two

Angels, both righteous and fallen, engage in military operations focused on framing the real nature of how all things came to be; their target, a small group of men and women whose core beliefs are challenged as the truth about origins is brought to light.

Major Questions Addressed:

1. How can the creation timeline of the Biblical account be reconciled with the cosmological timeline presented by the majority of contemporary scientists?
2. How can the theory of evolution be reconciled with a Biblical creation account which appears to preclude such from being a possibility if the Bible is accurate?
3. How can a fossil record which appears to present death as having occurred for much longer than 6000 years on the Earth be reconciled with the Biblical account of death only entering the world with the fall of Adam?

Created: Image Bearers – Book Three

As thousands of years of misunderstanding unravel amid the spiritual warfare being fought over the control of the story of creation, mankind's true origins rush to the surface, revealed in small pieces until their tale, that of the Image Bearers, finally is made known.

Major Questions Addressed:

1. Why does there appear to be a contradiction between the Biblical creation stories found in Genesis 1 and Genesis 2?
2. How does the story of the Sons of God found in Genesis 6 relate to the creation of mankind presented in Genesis 1?
3. How does the creation of mankind in Genesis 1, which is described as a special creation Biblically, fit with evolutionary scientist's story of mankind's origins through evolution from a common ancestor?

Created: Living Beings – Book Four

When the fall of the Image Bearers appears to validate aspects of Satan's accusations against God, the King provides a representative line to affirm the sentence against the fallen angels and provide a way of escape for fallen man; but, will that representative and his offspring fare any better than their predecessors?

Major Questions Addressed:

1. How can Adam and Eve be viewed as the first human beings when the fossil record and Human Genome Project demonstrate human origins dating much longer ago than 6000-10,000 years?
2. What role did Adam actually play as it pertains to the relationship between God and man?
3. How did Adam's fall condemn all of mankind to the effects of sin?

Created: The Remnant – Book Five

With both lines of men burdened with the same eternal destiny as the fallen angels, the accusations against God seemingly proven to be true, and by all appearances, no perceivable pathway to a different ending, Satan stands ready to claim his victory; but with God, all things are possible, and He always preserves a Remnant.

Major Questions Addressed:

1. What actually occurred with Noah's flood?
2. What actually took place with the story of the Tower of Babel?
3. Why is Abram's call not just the creation of the Hebrew race, but also the first step in God's reclamation of mankind as a whole?

Created: The God-Man – Book Six

How can God answer Satan's impossible accusation and save mankind from the destiny of the fallen angels? He is the way, the truth, and the life; no one comes to the Father except through the God-Man...Jesus.

Major Questions Addressed:

1. Why does the Bible say Jesus was crucified before the foundations of the world were laid?
2. How can a loving God really sacrifice His own Son to save mankind when He is omnipotent and supposedly able to do anything by any means?
3. How does Jesus' sacrificial death on the cross relate to God's initial creation of the Earth and mankind?

ABOUT THE AUTHOR

G regory A Rogers is a graduate of Baylor University in Waco, Texas and an entrepreneur who has worked in a variety of industries. Most recently, he served as the CEO of an online education company featuring 6th-12th grade curriculum written with a Biblical worldview. Prior to that, he worked for 27 years in various roles in healthcare including as CEO for several hospitals in Dallas, Texas. In addition to these accomplishments and his work on the Created series, Gregory recently gained recognition for his artwork including oil & acrylic painting, sidewalk chalk art, and theatrical stage sets and props. Most importantly to him, Gregory is a born-again Christian, married to Amanda since 1993, and the father of sons, Ryan and Jackson.

How could he ever dream of writing a book? At the time he began writing *Created: The Devil's Apprentice*, he was already engaged to develop and launch a new system of neurological rehabilitation hospitals. Despite the demands of that start-up effort, Greg found himself sitting in front of his computer, compelled to write about the beginning of all things. In 2013, Greg was approached by a friend who had recently walked away from Christianity. That friend challenged him to examine the origins of our universe and all it contains. He also asked Greg to review what he thought were contradictory claims in the Bible. In his opinion, if Greg did so, he too would walk away from Christianity.

Believing truth could stand up to scrutiny, Greg accepted the challenge and began studying the many perspectives on the subject. As he did, he noticed each group, believing themselves to be correct, discounted every challenge to their own position, even when those challenges seemed valid. Presuppositions clouded perspectives on every side, and discussions leaned towards upholding existing views rather than seeking truth. For the next 8 years, Greg listened to all sides, renewed his search through the Bible, and challenged every position. In the end, his faith in the God of the Bible grew. Now, in the Created series, Greg offers a fresh perspective, one which seems certain to capture the attention of both theists and atheists alike. "How far will God go to maintain His own perfection?" Will either side accept his theory?